# The Fair Folk
# and Little Orphan Mary

—— *A Tale about Gnomes* ——

"As a boy, I read Maria Konopnicka's classic fairy tale in the Polish original, and I was fascinated by it. Now, as an old man—thanks to Christopher Adam Zakrzewski's excellent translation—I have read this tale in English and am equally delighted by it. *The Fair Folk* is a story for both young and old, teaching the former, and reminding the latter, of the importance of discerning good and evil, of loving the earth and nature, of respecting honest labor, of empathizing with and helping the poor. Zakrzewski admirably captures the full scope of the author's genius, her enchanting storytelling, her wisdom, imagination, and sense of humor. He raises the Polish masterpiece to its rightful place on the Parnassus of world literature."

— Professor Kazimierz Braun, Polish writer and scholar

"The title of this moving tale evokes Hans Christian Andersen and his distinctive treatment of the fairy tale genre, but what is delivered here goes beyond the pattern popularized by the Danish author. Yes, the standard elements of nineteenth-century fairy tale are present: gnomes, queens, nature and its seasons, and a happy ending. But the gnomes have unmistakably Polish features, the orphan does not become a queen, society's problems are intensely present, and the show ends annually with the coming of winter.

"Konopnicka's tale is a joy to read. It can cheer up adults as well as children. Beautifully translated by arguably the best Polish-English translator alive, it belongs with Kenneth Grahame's *The Wind in the Willows*, Lewis Carroll's *Alice in Wonderland* and medieval morality plays. A mood-lifter and serenity summoner, it is a book to reach for when one needs a proclamation that 'all is (almost) right with the world.'"

— Ewa Thompson, Rice University

"This translation of Konopnicka's classic fairy tale is a true blessing not merely to a new generation of children who will be introduced to it for the first time but for all lovers of fantasy. As G. K. Chesterton reminds us in 'Ethics of Elfland' and as Tolkien insists in his seminal essay 'On Fairy-Stories', classic tales from the realm of Faërie offer a restorative to grown-ups in need of consolation and the recovery of a clearer view of reality.

— Joseph Pearce, author of *Tolkien: Man and Myth and/or Further Up and Further In: Understanding Narnia*

"For those who love fairy stories, and the folklore of Europe in general, this charming and deftly translated English edition of Maria Konopnicka's classic will offer numerous delights. Christopher Zakrzewski's poetic gifts are unsurpassed."

—Michael D. O'Brien, author of *Island of the World*

# The Fair Folk
# and Little Orphan Mary

—— *A Tale about Gnomes* ——

## Maria Konopnicka

Translated and adapted from the Polish
by Christopher Adam Zakrzewski

CHERRY ORCHARD BOOKS

2024

**Library of Congress Cataloging-in-Publication Data**

**Names:** Konopnicka, Maria, 1842-1910, author. | Zakrzewski, Christopher Adam, translator.

**Title:** The fair folk and little orphan Mary : a tale about gnomes / Maria Konopnicka ; translated and adapted from the Polish by Christopher Adam Zakrzewski.

**Other titles:** O krasnoludkach i sierotce Marysi. English

**Description:** Boston : Cherry Orchard Books, 2025. | Audience term: Preteens

**Identifiers:** LCCN 2024034209 (print) | LCCN 2024034210 (ebook) | ISBN 9798887196886 (hardback) | ISBN 9798887196893 (paperback) | ISBN 9798887196909 (adobe pdf) | ISBN 9798887196916 (epub)

**Subjects:** CYAC: Gnomes—Fiction. | Helpfulness—Fiction. | Spring--Fiction. | Orphans—Fiction. | Fairy tales. | LCGFT: Fairy tales.

**Classification:** LCC PZ8.K83 Fai 2025 (print) | LCC PZ8.K83 (ebook) | DDC [Fic]—dc23

LC record available at https://lccn.loc.gov/2024034209
LC ebook record available at https://lccn.loc.gov/2024034210

For my grandchildren

# Contents

# Translator's Preface

———

Like Kenneth Grahame's *The Wind in the Willows* and Antoine de Saint Exupéry's *Le Petit Prince,* Maria Konopnicka's *The Fair Folk and Little Orphan Mary* belongs to that rare number of children's books that appeal equally, if not more so, to the adult child. First published in 1896, it remains one of its nation's most frequently republished works, re-edited in millions of copies, and is standard reading in the first grades of Polish high schools. The tale has been translated into scores of languages including French, Italian, German, Russian, Ukrainian, Czech, Lithuanian, and Hebrew. A heavily abridged adaptation, long out of print, also exists in English.[1]

*The Fair Folk* is much more than a quaint story about Gnomes. Written in rich, lyrical prose, frequently shifting into the peasant dialect and interspersed with sundry verses and songs, the work is replete with mytho-folkloric motifs, legends, superstitions, historical and biblical references. The reader will find in it magical depictions of natural phenomena: the sunsets, the twilights, the changing seasons, the shadows, colors, sounds and silences, Poland's diverse landscape, her fields, forests and mountains, along with their flora and fauna; and realistic descriptions of late 19th-century Polish rural life.

———

1   See Kate Zuk-Skarszewska, *The Brownie Scouts* (Print Book, 1929).

Not least among *The Fair Folk*'s charms is the author's whimsical sense of humor—a humor that often rises to a level of high hilarity. In all this, Konopnicka "delights and instructs" in accordance with the classical principle of *docendi cum delectatione.*

The strong moralistic tone of the work must also be understood in the context of Poland's troubled and fractured history, particularly the period of her partitions (1772–1795) which resulted in the erasing of the sovereign state from the political map of Europe for over 120 years, until its reinstatement in 1918 by the terms of the Treaty of Versailles. Konopnicka was a representative of the Positivist movement: a social, literary, and philosophical movement that arose in late-19th-century partitioned Poland after the suppression of the second of two major insurrections against the Russian Empire occurring within a generation of each other (1830, 1863). The Positivists came to view "organic work" rather than uprisings, as the true path to preserving Polish national identity and affirming a constructive patriotism. Among the movement's societal concerns were the securing of equal rights for all members of society, including women and the peasantry; the integration of Poland's large Jewish minority (Konopnicka was considered a philosemite); the elimination of illiteracy resulting from closure of Polish schools by the partitioning powers; and defense of the Polish population in German-ruled Poland against Bismarck's *Kulturkampf* and displacing of Poles with German settlers. In Russian-ruled Poland, the festering "peasant question" was further aggravated by the emancipation of Russia's serfs in 1861.

*The Fair Folk* deals expressly with Poland's impoverished peasantry with whom the author evinced a particularly strong sense of solidarity. Perhaps nowhere in world literature— Władysław Reymont's monumental novel *The Peasants* (1897–1904) notwithstanding—can one find more viscerally poignant depictions of rural poverty. While the charge of sentimentalism is often leveled against many of Konopnicka's short stories and poems, such is the depth and sincerity of the sentiment expressed in *The Fair Folk* that the criticism here is rendered moot. In the words of the Polish poet Cyprian Norwid, the author, arguably, does not "drag truths down from the Heavens, but rather cries for them." Something similar might be said of Konopnicka's attitude to religious faith. While it is true that she was given to expressing anticlerical views (not an uncommon or altogether unhealthy corrective reaction in a traditionally Catholic country—her characterization of the unctuous hen-snatcher, Greasy Tod, might be seen as an expression of it) the sincere religious piety she imparts to her peasant characters points to a deeply held traditional Christian faith, one that belies the claims of today's progressivists who would appropriate the author as one of their own.

## A Note on the Treatment of Personal Names and Sundry Adaptations

My purpose here has been to render the classic as faithfully and with as little adaptation as possible. Englishing the gnomes' Polish names should ruffle no feathers. Attaching English names to non-human creatures is no greater a stretch than giving them Polish ones. A liberty has admittedly been taken in my treatment of the rest of the characters' names. This project was originally intended for my English-speaking grandchildren and sent to them in installments. There, wherever possible, I took the liberty of substituting the Christian names of the story's children with those of my grandchildren, and replacing the various Polish surnames with shorter ones less daunting to the English reader, most of which I gleaned from current Polish newspapers. When the scope of the English readership widened, I saw no reason not to keep those names. In addition, I have toned down a few instances in the text which, while sociologically accurate, might offend against modern sensibilities. Apart from these minor adaptations, the integrity of the original text has been scrupulously preserved.

Christopher Adam Zakrzewski

A fairy tale, you say?
Think what you like, but I
Insist that Gnomes exist!
You'll find them everywhere.

> Quaint, tiny little folk,
> Like fine seeds in a pod.
> Sheer make-believe, you say?
> Just ask old Nannykins!

Gnome-folk dwell in the hills,
In hollows, under stones,
Beneath the stove, the sills,
In any vacant mousehole.

> Open the spence a crack,
> You'll see them scampering there;
> Sometimes they turn the spit
> Behind Aunt Sophie's back.

A crackling picce goes missing?
The sugar loaf gets gnawed?
A dinner scrap brushed off
The table—vanishes?

> Who snarled old Chestnut's mane?
> Who cracked the whip? Why, Gnomes!
> They stuff your wee ones' heads
> With tales. Oh! charming tales!

No nook's too small, no whim
Too wild; they flit like shadows.
There's no denying Gnomes,
Sharp, sprightly little beggars!

But then think as you please,
Deny it if you will,
I still say Gnomes exist —
Just ask old Nannykins!

# 1

# How King Glistel's Court Chronicler Discovered Spring

———

The bitterly cold winter dragged on for so long that His Gracious Majesty Glistel, the Gnome King, froze fast to his throne. His gray beard, stiff with icicles, turned a hoary silver, and his snow-capped eyebrows took on a grim, forbidding aspect. Instead of pearls, the crown upon his head sparkled with frozen dewdrops, and his condensing breath settled like snow on the crystal walls of his rocky grotto. His loyal subjects the sprightly Gnomes sought whatever comfort they could in their red mantles and ample hoods. Many sewed warm vests and overcoats for themselves from materials gathered in the woodland that autumn: green and russet mosses, pine-cone seeds, shelf-fungus skin, squirrels' fur, and even feathers shed by the departing birds.

But a king could scarcely go about appareled in so rude and common a fashion. Winter and summer, Glistel was fain to wear the purple robe which had served the Gnome Kings for centuries untold. By now it was quite worn, and you could feel the wind whistling through it. Truth to tell, Glistel had never found the garment very warm, not even in his earliest days as king. Woven from yarn spun by the tiny red spiders that scamper about the garden beds in spring, the fabric had scarcely the thickness of a poppy petal.

So the King shivered mightily. Now and again he blew on his nails, for his fingers grew so numb that his royal scepter would slip from their grasp. Of course, there was no question of lighting a fire in a crystal palace. You'd only end up cracking everything, the parquet tiles, the walls . . .

So King Glistel warmed himself by the glow of his gold and silver hoard, by the flames of his diamonds (large as larks' eggs!), by the rainbows that fugitive beams of sunlight formed on the crystal walls of his throne room, and by the sparks glancing off the long swords that his brave Gnomes exercised with—as much to stay warm as to display their native courage. But all these things gave off very little heat, so little, in fact, that the wretched King's few remaining teeth chattered violently. And so he longed impatiently for spring.

"Firebrand, my faithful servant!" said he to one of his attendants. "Go out into the world and look for signs of spring."

But Firebrand humbly replied:

"My Lord King, I never venture into the world until the nettles by the peasant's fence turn green, and that won't be for a good while yet."

The King shook his head, then shaking it again said:

"Titmouse, perhaps you'll have a look?"

But neither was Titmouse keen to poke his nose out in the frost.

"My Lord King," said he, "I never venture into the world until the wagtails start to peep, and we aren't nearly there yet."

For a while the King said nothing, but as the frost continued to nip at his fingers, he shook his head yet again, and said:

"Maribeetle, my faithful servant, would *you* mind taking a look outside?"

But even Maribeetle wasn't eager to brave the wind and cold; he, too, bowed and said:

"My Lord King, I never venture into the world until the drowsy midge stirs under the sear leaf, and that isn't for a while yet."

Glistel's head dropped to his chest. He sighed, and with that sigh there burst forth such a swirl of snow that for a time you could make nothing out in the Grotto.

A week passed, two weeks passed, then one morning it became a little brighter, and the icicles on the King's beard began to melt. The snow-caps on his head and royal eyebrows shrank, and the melted ice beading his whiskers dripped like tears from his chin.

Before long even the walls began to thaw, cracking and booming like the mighty Vistula[1] river. Soon, it became so damp in the cavern that the King and his attendants were sneezing like banging drums.

Now please note that Gnomish noses are no mean endowments. True, Gnomes are not very big. When one sees a peasant's boot, he stands up straight and gapes in amazement, for he thinks he's standing before the town hall. When he

---

1 Poland's principal river, which takes its source in the Carpathian Mountains and flows north into the Baltic Sea.

clambers into the hen house, he says, "Now there's a city for you! Which way to the turnpike?" And when he falls into a quart vessel, he yells, "Help! I'm drowning in the well!" That's how small they are.

But a Gnome's nose is a splendid affair. The parish organist couldn't boast of a better to snort his snuff with. And so when the King and all his court fired off a salvo of sneezes and followed it up with choruses of "BLESS YOU!"—oh my! how the earth shook. A peasant who happened to be gathering firewood in the forest would hear the sneezing and say to himself, "Oho! Thunder! Winter's breathing his last!" (He'd take the noise for a spring storm.) At once he'd turn his nag toward the nearest inn (why waste another groat on firewood!) and bide there till sunset, reckoning up what needed doing before next year's snowfall.

Meanwhile, the thaw was blowing great guns. By noon every Gnome's beard had become unfrozen.

They began to discuss whom they should send out into the world. At last, King Glistel tapped the ground with his golden scepter, and announced:

"Our learned chronicler Fiddle-Fuddle shall go out and see if spring has sprung."

"Wise choice, Your Majesty!" cried the Gnomes. All eyes turned on the learned Gnome Fiddle-Fuddle.

The old chronicler was busy as usual poring over the great clasped tome in which he recorded all that had passed in the Gnomish kingdom from ancient times on: where the Fair Folk hailed from, their line of kings, the wars they'd fought and how they fared in them. Whatever he'd seen and heard he set down faithfully, and what he hadn't seen or heard, he embroidered so beautifully that the hearts of all who read it fairly burst with pride. It was he who proved beyond the shadow of a doubt that Gnomes, who stood barely an inch high, were really giants who'd shrunk themselves so as to save on cloth for their vests and cloaks, since everything was so costly.

The Gnomes were very proud of their chronicler; so much so, that whenever they came across an unknown herb, they'd weave it at once into a garland and bind his brow with it. In time, these coronals wore away the few remaining hairs on his head, and now it was as bald as my knee-cap.

* * *

Fiddle-Fuddle lost no time in preparing himself for his expedition. He found himself a large pot of the blackest ink, then trimmed a very large goose quill (the pen was so heavy he had to shoulder it like a rifle); his bulky old books he strapped to his back, then girding his traveling cloak with a leather belt he donned his hood and wooden clogs, lit a long-stemmed pipe, and thus fitted out, stood ready to embark on his journey.

The Chronicler's loyal companions began wishing him tearful farewells. Who knew what perilous adventures awaited him in the world, or if, indeed, they'd ever see him again?

King Glistel, who was very fond of his learned scholar, rose to embrace him. Alas! His stiff robes stuck stubbornly to the throne and held him down; so, raising his golden scepter he waved it majestically over the scholar's head. When Fiddle-Fuddle kissed his hand, several bright pearls (the good King's frozen tears) rolled down the royal face and fell with a tinkling sound to the crystal floor. At once Chancellor of the Exchequer Groatkin seized them up, and dropping them into a precious jewel case carried them off to the treasury.

It took a whole day of heavy climbing for the learned Gnome to reach the mouth of the Grotto. The way was steep and blocked with the roots of ancient oaks. Rocks, gravel and brash broke loose underfoot and fell ricocheting into the abyss below. Frozen waterfalls covered stretches of the ledge with clear sheets of ice, and over these the traveler's wooden-clogged feet slithered and slid. So it was with great difficulty that he trekked his way upward.

To make matters worse, Fiddle-Fuddle had set out on his journey without packing any provisions. The enormous weight of the books, ink-pot and pen ruled out carrying anything else. Certainly he would have dropped from sheer exhaustion had he not stumbled upon the well-supplied home of a prudent vole.

The vole had a larder full of grain and beech-nuts, and of this ample store he gave the starving wayfarer to eat. He even allowed him to make his bed in the hay he'd strewn over the floor of his burrow—all this on the strict condition that no one in the village should learn of his whereabouts.

"For—said he—there's nasty little boys about, and if they found out where I lived, well, I'd never know another moment's peace. And that's a fact!"

Next morning, refreshed in body and mind, Fiddle-Fuddle bade the kind vole farewell and resumed his journey. Striking a brisk, jaunty pace, he began to peer out of his dark hood and take notice of the peasants' field-plots, the meadows and groves. Tender green shoots were sprouting everywhere: young grasses sprang up in the damp hollows; splashes of red appeared on the willow sprays that overhung the swollen stream; and high up in the quiet misty air you could hear the cry of cranes on the wing.

Any other Gnome would have recognized these signs of spring at once, but Fiddle-Fuddle had been so absorbed in books since his youth that he knew nothing of the world; indeed, he had little understanding of anything at all.

Even so, he was seized by such a strange sense of inner joy and levity of heart that all at once he began waving his great pen about and broke out into a popular old ditty:

> *Bothers hence! Cares begone!*
> *Pack your pipe, quaff a pint . . .*

He was partway into the stave when he heard the sound of birds chirping. Looking up, he saw a flock of raucous sparrows perched on a wattle fence enclosing a small field. Loath to be seen joining in with this rifffraff, Fiddle-Fuddle broke off singing, frowned, and passed them by with an air of great gravity; clearly, learned folk held no truck with common house sparrows.

By and by, spying a peasant village, he swung off the path and struck out onto ground overgrown with last year's weeds; and so he arrived unseen at the first cottage.

The large sprawling village stood surrounded by fruit trees that hung still bare and leafless. The furthest dwellings backed onto the dark wall of a dense pine forest. The settlement had a prosperous look. Its cottages were freshly whitewashed; wreaths of blue smoke rose from the chimneys. In the yards outside you could hear the creaking of the wooden sweep as the farm lads watered the horses and lowing cattle. Noisy groups of children played tag and hide-and-seek in the poplar-lined street.

Hammer blows and the clang of beaten iron resounded in the nearby forge; a group of village women stood gathered around it. Fiddle-Fuddle crept up along a wooden fence and listened intently from behind a sloeberry bush.

"The thieving bandit!" cried one of the women. "Now that he's broken into the smith's hen-house, there won't be a banty safe anywhere."

"Banty, my eye!" snorted her neighbor. "Mine was pure gold! Laying eggs day after day, as big as your fist. You won't find the like in the whole village!"

"And who throttled the life out of my rooster," said another. Was that his doing too? When I saw those scattered feathers I near fainted with grief, see if I didn't! A silver florin he'd have fetched me, and fifteen groats into the bargain!"

"The scoundrel!" said the first woman. "Some cat! Some paws! Fancy burrowing under the hen-house like that! A strong lad with a spade couldn't do better. No thief could have done it!"

Suddenly, the blacksmith's wife minus her pinafore burst out of the cottage, and raising her apron to her eyes, not minding the cold, began wailing loudly:

"Oh, my dear little birds! My golden cockerels! Now what'll become of me, bereft as I am?"

Astonished and puzzled by these cries, Fiddle-Fuddle listened first with one ear then the other. Then, suddenly, tapping his brow with his finger, he sat down among the weeds by the fence, uncorked his ink-pot, dipped in his quill, gave it a flourish, and opening his great book set down the following:

"On the second day of my journey, I came upon an unhappy region recently marauded by the Golden Horde.[2] The Tartars killed a good many of its hens and roosters and took the rest into captivity, and so the blacksmith was forging swords for an armed foray. And all around there was great wailing and loud lamentation."

He was still scribbling this down when the blacksmith stepped out of the forge and cried out in a deep voice.

"What's the use of this wailing! What we need is a pan of coals. Smoke the villain out! Obviously, there's a fox lurking in the forest. Smoke him out, or dig him out. Step lively, Stas! Quick, Jan! Call the boys, get a spade and go after him! And you, Mother, stop your squawking! Go fetch a pan of coals! I'd do it myself, only I've pressing work to do."

Saying which he strode back to the forge, and the clang of iron resounded again. Meanwhile, the blacksmith's lads dropped the bellows and raced through village, crying, "Smoke out the fox! Smoke out the fox!"

The women ran back to their cottages to prepare for the expedition.

Fiddle-Fuddle, sharp-eyed as ever, dipped in his pen again and wrote down in his book:

---

2   A body of Mongols, also known as Tartars, that overran Eastern Europe and parts of Eurasia in the thirteenth century and dominated the area until 1486.

"These Tartars have a fearless leader, a Khan called The Great Fox; they hide in dugouts in the forest whence the local populace must drive them out with cannon-smoke."

Scarcely had the learned chronicler set down these lines when a frightful tumult fell upon his ears. Looking up, he saw rushing past him a great throng of village women, youngsters and little children armed with saucepans, spades and sticks; behind them ran a motley raggle-taggle pack of housedogs, barking and howling furiously. Away they went in the direction of the forest. Once again Fiddle-Fuddle dipped in his pen and added this note to his chronicle:

"In this land it is not menfolk that go to war with the Tartars, but the women, children and youngsters. When marching on the enemy, this host raises a terrible hue and cry. They charge through the village at great speed, and behind the main troop follows a pack of hounds whose dreadful cry cheers them to the assault."

Here, lowering his head, he squinted his left eye, and signing "Fiddle-Fuddle, Court Historian of His Majesty, King Glistel" in the corner of the page, he graced the signature with a bold, elaborate flourish.

Meanwhile, there came wafting from the other side of the fence the pleasant smell of juniper smoke—something Gnomes especially liked. Fiddle-Fuddle sniffed his prodigious nose once, then twice, then parting the tall weed-stalks looked to see where the smoke was coming from. A wreath of blue smoke was rising into the air by the pine forest yonder. Giving his spectacles a good wipe, he saw a small bonfire in the field, and around it sat a small group of shepherd children. Now the kind Gnome was very fond of children, and so guiding his steps by the thread of smoke, he set out across the fallow ground, cheerfully leaping the furrows toward the bonfire.

Upon catching sight of a tiny hooded manikin with a great book under his arm, an ink-pot under his leather belt, and a goose quill over his shoulder, the children were sorely amazed.

Little Jacob Lis nudged his cousin Tristek Grot with his elbow, and pointing his finger at the little creature whispered:

"A Gnome!"

Drawing closer to the children, Fiddle-Fuddle smiled and nodded in a friendly manner. The children stared open-mouthed at him, as though they'd seen a rainbow. They felt no trace of fear, only a sudden sense of awe. For, children know perfectly well that Gnomes do nobody any harm, and even like to help out poor little orphans. Jacob recalled how last spring the heifers under his care had strayed into the forest and how one such little fellow had helped him to find them and drive them back into the meadow. The Gnome even stroked his head and dropped a handful of wild strawberries into his hat, saying: "Don't be afraid! Here, take these, little waif!"

Meanwhile, approaching the fire, Fiddle-Fuddle took his pipe out of his mouth and said politely:

"Good afternoon, little children!"

"Good afternoon, sir!" replied the boys earnestly.

But the girls only huddled up to each other, and drawing their kerchiefs over their foreheads so you could barely see the tips of their noses, they gawked at the guest with their corn-flower-blue eyes.

Fiddle-Fuddle smiled at them.

"May I warm myself by your fire?" he asked. "It's rather chilly!"

"Of course you may, sir!" said Jacob Lis resolutely.

"We don't mind!" blurted out his sister Emily, the most forward of the girls.

"Oh, please sit down, sir!" said Tristek. Here's a nice spot!"

And drawing up the skirts of his little gray caftan he made room for him by the fire.

"We're baking taters, and you can share with us if you like," said Jacob's other sister Maryna hospitably.

Others piped up:

"Yes do, sir! See, they're almost ready. You can tell by the smell."

Fiddle-Fuddle sat down with the children and gazed sweetly at their glowing little faces.

"Oh, my dear children!" he said tenderly. "But how can I repay you?"

He'd scarcely uttered these words when Tristek's sister Kasia, covering her eyes with her hand, blurted forth:

"You could tell us a fairy tale . . ."

"Ah, what's a fairy tale!" said her brother in a serious tone. "The truth's always better than a fairy tale."

"Of course, of course it's better!" said Fiddle-Fuddle. "There's nothing better than the truth."

"Well, if that's so," piped up little Nathan Lasek, "then tell us how the Gnomes came into this world."

"How they came into this world?" said Fiddle-Fuddle, and he was about to begin his tale when the potato skins suddenly began to burst open with a series of loud explosions. At once the children leapt up, sticks in hand, and began digging them out of the embers and ashes.

Terrified by these sudden detonations, the learned scholar started up and sought shelter behind a field stone. From his stronghold there, he raised his head and observed the children gobbling down some round, smoking objects he didn't recognize; whereupon, opening his book, he leaned on the field stone and with trembling hand wrote down these words:

"The people of this land are so hardy and war-like that their little children bake live ordnance in the hot ashes. Heated by the embers, these shells begin to burst with a roar, loud as thunder in the sky. Then their boys who are raised to scorn death from very infancy, and even their delicate little girls, dig out these exploding shells and pop them still smoking into their mouths. Of which fact, I, an eyewitness and one unable to marvel enough at such knightly animus, make note for the lasting memory of our descendants. Recorded in a fallow field, around tea-time."

Meanwhile, there spread over the field such a delicious aroma of baked potatoes that the learned Gnome became suddenly aware of the great emptiness in his belly. Seeing that no harm came to the children from eating these bursting shells and that they were even rubbing their tummies with delight at this enticing fare, he crept out from behind the stone and approached the fire. At once Emily Lis broke up a potato and offered him a morsel on the tip of a little stick. Not without trepidation did Fiddle-Fuddle reach for that morsel, but as soon as he'd tasted it, he put out his hand for more. The little girl crumbled the most perfectly baked potato and began offering it to him piece by piece. Soon they'd all grown so used to the Gnome that Emily popped the last tidbit into his mouth herself, whereupon they all squealed with excruciating delight—her youngest sister Jasia loudest among them.

* * *

After eating his fill, the learned Gnome resumed his place by the fire, and when the boys had heaped on more branches and the sparks leapt merrily up from the dry twigs, he began telling them about the Gnomes.

"In olden times we were called Godlets. We didn't live as we do now, underground, under rocks or the roots of ancient trees, but in villages with human folk. That was a long, long time ago! Old King Lech[3] was still ruling over the land then. He founded the castle town of Gnesna[4] on the spot where he saw great flocks of white birds building their nests. For, he said to himself, 'If these birds live here in safety, then the land must be good, and free from strife.'

"And so it was.

"People say those white birds were eagles, but our old books clearly state they were storks that thronged the lowland meadows and built their nests there. It was as it was! Enough that this whole land took its name from King Lech, and those living in it became known as the People of Lech. Their neighbors also called them the Polans, since they were tillers of the fields,

---

3   Lech was the mythical progenitor of the Poles, even as his brothers Czech and Rus were the progenitors of the Bohemians and Russians, respectively.

4   The Latin name for Gniezno, the first historical capital of Poland in the tenth century and early eleventh century.

workers of plowshares. All this stands written under seal in our old books."

"So weren't there any forests then?" piped up Nathan in a thin voice. "Or rivers, or anything?"

"Oh, indeed there were!" replied Fiddle-Fuddle. "There was a forest, not like the one yonder but a rude and fearful wilderness, almost boundless! In it lurked a fierce beast whose loud roars would shatter the frailer trees. But we Gnomes know only about the bears. The great-grandsire of my great-great-grandfather told me how a bear once scooped him up along with a swarm of honey bees from a cleft in a linden-tree and kept him captive in his den for half the winter, making him tell stories day and night while he sucked on his paw and dozed. Not until the keenest frost had set in and the bear was snoring soundly did my great-great-grandfather's great-grandsire manage to escape and, after seven years of trekking through the wilderness, return to our people."

The children laughed on hearing this tale. Fiddle-Fuddle went on:

"Ho! Ho! ... Yes indeed, those were the days! ... Once upon a time, there were linden groves murmuring over these fields and rivers. Among these groves there lived an old, old god named Svetovid,[5] who faced the world in three directions and protected the land.

"The households, livestock and farmyards—these were looked after by us Godlets, whom human folk also called Gnomes because of our small size.

---

5   Svetovid: literally, "world watcher."

"'Every home has its Gnome,' they used to say. Oh, we had it good then, and we were happy to help our hosts in all manner of work. We would fill the horses' nosebags, winnow the chaff, so that only the golden grain remained; we'd cut the straw and mix it with hay, chase the hens back into the yard, so that they wouldn't get lost in the nettles; we'd churn the butter, press the cheese, rock the babies in their cradles, reel the yarn, and blow into the fire to heat up the groats quicker. True, we didn't do this for nothing. If the master of the house forgot us, the mistress was sure to remember. Bread crumbs or cheese curds would always be left on the edge of the bench in the parlor. Always there was honey or milk left in a cup. We never went lacking. When going out to weed the kitchen garden or harvest the cornfield, the mistress would look around the hut, scoop up millet seed from the barrel and scatter it over the floor, saying:

> *Little Folk! Little Folk!*
> *Mind my waifs, keep them safe!*
> *A cup of meal for your zeal!*

"And thus reassured she'd go off to work. Meanwhile, zip! from under the brick stove, zip! from under the bench, zip! from under the painted blanket box we'd come darting out and set to work: we'd tidy the parlor, amuse the tots with tales, plane hobbyhorses for the boys, knit dolls for the girls and braid their hair; we'd clean the windows, open them wide to let in the sun, so as to brighten every nook of the hut and make everything fresh! There was work aplenty, no denying, but our hosts couldn't thank us enough. No marriage was arranged, no young lad's ceremonial haircut took place without their inviting us Gnomes:

> *Little Folk! Little Folk!*
> *Join us wights, share some bites!*
> *Bison-flesh, lean and fresh,*
> *Fowl, deer-meat, round-cake sweet.*

"Of course, it wasn't our habit to go pushing in among the guests, for, though small, we Gnomes are discreet. Instead, two, three or even ten of us would gather by the window or door and strike up tunes on our *gusli*[6] strings. The guests couldn't hear enough of our little band! Such merriment! Such joy! Such heartfelt singing and dancing! Hey! Hey! Oh, where did those good times go?!"

* * *

Fiddle-Fuddle paused and puffed slowly on his pipe. The children, all eyes and ears, never stirred.

"How long it lasted," he resumed, "I couldn't say, for our books are silent on the matter. But times began to change. Good masters grew scarcer in the Land of Lech; and those that came after them were always bickering and at loggerheads with each other. Finally, growing tired of these quarrelers, the people drove them out and settled on one lord.

---

6   A multi-string plucked instrument belonging to the zither family.

"Peace returned, but the sun had scarcely time to shine on the land when there broke another storm.

"Like a swarm of locusts reducing the grain to stubble, the Teutons fell upon our fields and laid them waste. Their over-lord had a mind to wed our lady and become master of our land. I say '*our* land,' because in those still pristine days, we Gnomes and human folk were like brothers. We lived as one. Anyway, the lady refused to marry the Teutonic prince—"

"Oh, I know!" cried out Maryna in a thin voice. "That was Wanda!"[7]

"Oh, I know, too!" squealed Jasia Lis in an even thinner voice.

And at once the two girls chanted out together:

"Wanda lies buried in our land; she wouldn't wed the Teuton lord . . ."

"No, she wouldn't!" said Fiddle-Fuddle, smiling and nod-ding his head. "I know! Quite right! . . . You can find the whole song in our books. We've been teaching it to village children since time out of mind. Why, I must have taught a hundred tots myself! How did you learn it?"

"Oh, *we* don't know!"

"Then it must have been *me*! The second time you hear it, it's like something in the air speaking or singing to you."

"That's true!" said the boys earnestly.

"There, you see? It's Gnomes speaking and singing to you like that, but since they're so small, you don't see them hiding in the cornfield or the meadow grass, or in the groves, among the leaves, or beneath a field stone.

---

7 A legendary Polish warrior-queen of the eighth century, a time when Poland was under threat from the much stronger German host.

"Now, where was I? Oh yes! So, when the lady refused the hand of the Teutonic prince, war broke out. Suddenly, ravens and crows began circling over the land. Wolves howled in the night, and jet clouds darkened the sky.

"We began to go hungry, as all the bread and cheese went to the warriors fighting the Teutons. Famine gripped the land, and we Gnomes suffered along with everyone else. Finally, grieved to no end by the war ravaging the land, our lady leapt into the Vistula and drowned herself. Only then did the Teutons leave the land, and peace returned.

"But war had so disjointed the times that it was all for naught! Brother betrayed brother, strong oppressed weak, the greedy seized the orphaned parcels of land. Where there is injury, where orphans' tears flow, there can be no happiness. A wicked line of rulers came to power—the Popielids."

"Lawks!" cried out Emily. *"Popielids?"*

"What are you squealing for?" bridled Jacob Lis. "You've heard of the Popielids! You know—*Poh-pyel,*[8] the one that got eaten up by mice."

"Right!" said Nathan Lasek with great seriousness.

But Fiddle-Fuddle, puffing out a plume of smoke, went on:

"People say all kinds of things about those mice—now this, now that. It was a long time ago, and no one today will get to the bottom of it. But it stands written in our books that it

---

8   Popiel was a legendary ninth-century ruler of two proto-Polish tribes, the Goplans and West Polans. He was the last member the Popielids, a mythical dynasty before the Piasts. According to the chronicler Gallus Anonymus and others, as a consequence of his bad rule he was deposed, besieged by his subjects, and eaten alive by mice in a tower overlooking Lake Goplo in Kruszwica.

wasn't mice at all, but us Gnomes dressed in mouse-skin coats, for the winter was very harsh, and, seeing that this Popiel was such a wicked ruler, they came out of the mouseholes in force, fell on him, and worried him to death.

"That's what our books say. Whether it's true or not is hard to say, but my great-great-grandfather told me that before he went blind with old age he saw that terrible lake and the grim keep in which all this is said to have taken place. The keep still stands today and bears the name Mouse Tower, and the lake is called Lake Goplo.

"So there you are!"

Here Fiddle-Fuddle began poking in the ashes for a glowing ember, Finding one, he relit his extinguished pipe, then pulling several times on the stem and letting out great puffs of smoke went on.

"That's the way it is with old books. A few leaves are missing, another few are so yellowed and faded you cannot read them; big black streaks run down or across others, so you can't know everything that was written down so many centuries ago.

"But you can tell at once if the times were good or bad! If they were good, then no matter how old and faded the page, a brightness shines out of it like the rising sun; if bad, an impenetrable darkness lies over it, as when, on a black night, even the moon and the stars are blotted out.

"That's what the Gnomes' old books are like!"

\* \* \*

"Do you want me to go on?" said Fiddle-Fuddle after pausing to re-light his pipe.

"Oh yes, yes!" cried out the girls.

"Good! Now listen! Right after those dark pages about Popiel come the bright pages telling of the wheelwright Piast.[9] Ho! Ho! . . . About this wheelwright, I could talk for hours."

At this little Nathan's eyes lit up.

"Oh my! Do tell!"

"Yes, do! Tell us everything you know!" cried the children excitedly.

Fiddle-Fuddle drew back his hood, scratched his bald crown, and resumed his tale:

"Here I cannot say much from first-hand knowledge, for I wasn't born yet. But an old Gnome who chronicled those times knew an oak-tree even older than himself who remembered them well. Though his voice had been reduced to a mere whisper, when he began murmuring of this wheelwright there fell over the whole wilderness a hush so deep you could have heard a poppy seed drop. And then the pine-trees, the spruces, the hornbeams, the beeches, the birches, and even the grasses and mosses and ferns would listen so raptly that not a leaf or blade of grass would utter a sigh.

"And so, murmuring, murmuring ever so softly, the venerable old oak would hold forth quietly and recall the days of his distant youth.

"The Gnome, who was still very young then—indeed, he was scarcely bigger than a titmouse—would seat himself under an accommodating mushroom. And thus he came to know the whole story, which he later set down in our books.

---

9   The House of Piast was the first historical ruling dynasty of Poland. The first documented Polish monarch was Duke Mieszko I (c. 960–992).

"Here's how it went:

The oak, a mere sapling then, stood among a stand of oaks, and not far off in the shade of a linden grove buzzing with honey bees there stood a bright larch cottage with three inhabitants: the wheelwright Piast, his wife Rorippa, and their golden-haired son whom they named Siemovit,[10] because he loved to look at the fields, and every day upon stepping out of the cottage he'd cry out, 'Greetings, fair Earth!'

"The oak would watch these three hard-working tender souls go about their daily labors, their hearts so pure you'd think each had a white dove in their breast.

"There were Gnomes living in the larch cottage as well, and they had it very nice there, for the wheelwright and his family shared everything they had with them: golden honey, white round-cake, the whitest cheeses; and thanks to their hard work, the household enjoyed abundance and plenty. A king's palace couldn't have done better than this bright, quiet cottage redolent of resin.

"Now the day came for the son to have his ceremonial haircut. Neighbors arrived for the occasion, some on foot, some in carts, others on unbroken colts, and the wheelwright's homestead thronged with guests.

"He and Rorippa bustled about, doing the honors, serving the guests, and the household Gnomes helped out the whole day long. But just as the sun was setting, there broke over the

---

10 Derived from words *siemo* (family) and *vit* (ruler, to rule). The name may also mean "head of the family." The author seems to have confused the name with Svetovid, deriving from the words *svet* (world) and *vid* (watcher, to watch).

cottage the strains of such divine singing that the people gazed up thinking the voices came from heaven.

"But the Gnomes turned suddenly pale, and even though it was a warm May evening, they began to shiver, as if a chill wind had passed over them.

"A Gnome hastening to serve a guest froze in his tracks and began to shake all over so that even his teeth chattered.

"Meanwhile, there appeared from out of the west, resplendent in the broad beams of the setting sun, two shining wayfarers; they were making for the wheelwright's cottage, and theirs were the singing voices.

"So strong, so sweet was their singing you'd swear that all the nightingales thronging the poplars in the garden were trilling; that all the dewdrops beading the herbs and field flowers were chiming like bells; that all the delicate linden leaves in the wheelwright's bee-garden were rustling, and all the corn and grasses in the fields were caroling with vibrant silver voices.

"The two shining wayfarers sang of how a time was ending in the land and a new era was beginning; of how the old gods whose carved images stood in the sacred groves would die and fall to dust, and a great Lord—the Lord of heaven and earth— would come in their stead.

"The people listened raptly to this singing, and strength and hope shone in their faces. But the Gnomes, recovering from their initial fright, hid themselves away in the darkest corner of the wheelwright's pantry where they huddled together, trembling like autumn leaves about to fall from the boughs. From their grandsires' grandfathers they had heard of a song that would come from the West announcing the advent of a great and powerful lord, the Lord of Heaven and Earth, and it would be a sign that they must forsake the larch cottage and yield their place to such shining winged spirits as had now appeared.

"In vain Rorippa bestrewed the parlor floor with poppy seeds and cake crumbs. Though hungry, the Gnomes were loath to come out and partake of the gifts. One old Gnome nudged the door open a crack and took a peek into parlor but then instantly covered his eyes with his hands, for the wayfarers' garments shone with such radiance it seemed as if the sun had entered the room.

"For many days and many nights the Gnomes sat cold and hungry in the pantry. Only when the radiance subsided and the song filling the air around the cottage fell silent did they finally venture out to serve the household as usual. But then they saw the wheelwright! A golden robe draped his coarse linen caftan, a shining circlet adorned his brow, and he was mounting a king's throne where no longer was he to be served by the Gnomes but by knights and noblemen.

"Rorippa, too, had become a queen, and Siemovit a prince. And so ended their freeholders' life in a cottage, and began their kingly life in what eventually became a castle.

"Loath to forsake the dear cottage where they'd spent so many happy, peaceful years, the Gnomes continued to reel the housemistress's yarn and mind the livestock, fields, and bee-hives.

"But they no longer set about these chores with the same zeal and address. The King's spencer[11] would leave milk and honey on the edge of the bench as had Rorippa before him,

---

11  Minder of the royal spence or pantry.

but the Gnomes refused to approach the food, for they felt themselves undeserving and their help to be of little use. Eating only the scraps that fell from the table, they grew so meager and wasted that instead of Godlets, the people started to call them The Poor Folk.

"Meanwhile, the strains of the divine song began to echo throughout the land, and when the crepuscular light spread across the western sky, something in the air would start to play and sing like a silver lyre. Some there were who could hear the words of this song:

> *Great and mighty comes the Lord . . .*
> *Lord of heaven and earth . . .*

"But to hear this, you needed a heart as pure as the early morning light. So murmured, so spoke the ancient oak, and all the while the wilderness listened in rapt silence . . ."

\* \* \*

Fiddle-Fuddle fell silent; the children sat silent, too, for it seemed to them they could hear the oak-tree's voice among the whispering pines. After a while little Nathan Lasek spoke up:

"And the Gnomes? What happened to them?"

But the ancient Gnome, lost in his musings over the old times, remained silent. The children began to tug at his cloak and call out to him.

"Tell us, dear Gnome! Do tell us! What happened to the little people?"

Roused from his thoughts, Fiddle-Fuddle resumed:

"For a while longer the Poor Folk went on living in the huts and villages, but they grew increasingly sadder, weaker and smaller. People no longer called as often on their help. While the King was alive, he saw to it that they came to no harm, and when his son succeeded him the Poor Folk still had their own little corner in every cottage. But by the time Siemovit's grandson took the throne, they'd so fallen out of grace that they no longer dared show themselves in the daytime and only ventured from their corner at dusk, to forage for food.

"Mothers, going out to work in the fields, no longer scattered millet for the Poor Folk; instead, they made the sign of the cross over the cottage. Scarcely would they close the door when the parlor would fill with light and the flutter of angels' wings. And so it was the angels who minded the tots. The Poor Folk were left only with the most menial of chores in the stable and cow-shed. In the house, they split kindling wood, washed the pots, and swept the dust into the corner.

"Then—as it states in the old books—came the day when the bells began to ring forth from the church towers. The peals rolled like thunder over the land, and wherever they were heard the Poor Folk left the cottages and villages in little groups, weeping and bidding the human settlements good-bye. They fled into the forests, into the mountains, into the meadows where the sound of the bells never reached.

"Since then human folk no longer see them except perhaps at night, and in the daytime it's the little children that see them, just as you see me now. Most of the Gnomes fled to the Southern Mountains,[12] where they watch over their buried hoard. A good number also fled into the forests, and because winter in the wilds is harsh, they made hooded cloaks for themselves and bright red caps that make them easy to recognize; hence the name Fair Folk[13] by which they are known today. Even now Gnomes have lost none of their affection for human folk: for a morsel of food, a spoonful of milk, they're only too happy to look after a loving household. But when they hear the sound of the church bells, they must hide underground . . . before the Great and Mighty Lord . . . the Lord of heaven and earth . . ."

Just as Fiddle-Fuddle was uttering these words, bowing his head reverently, a great commotion arose from out by the forest.

It was the village women and children returning from their hunting expedition. Alas, their return was not a jubilant one, for the cunning fox had many earths. By the time they'd dug up the first in the forest, he'd moved on to a second or third in the field among a clump of sloeberry bushes and hid himself there without a trace. The women were loudly lamenting the precious time wasted, and the children were calling back the dogs who were casting furiously for a scent along the edges of the forest.

On hearing the commotion, the shepherd children raised their heads and became so absorbed by the sights

---

12 That is, the Tatra Mountains; part of the Carpathian mountain chain that creates a natural border between Slovakia and Poland.

13 The Polish word for "gnome" is *krasnoludek*, deriving from the words *krasny*, formerly meaning both "red" and "beautiful," and *ludek*, "little human being."

and sounds that they forgot all about the Gnome. At this Fiddle-Fuddle started back from the fire, pulled up his hood, and leaping into a furrow vanished into last year's grasses, so that neither Tristek, nor Kasia, nor Jacob, nor Emily, nor Maryna nor Jasia, nor Nathan, nor even his little sisters Natalia and Amelia knew for sure if a Gnome had sat with them by the bonfire in the field and plied them with such marvelous tales.

* * *

Meanwhile, Fiddle-Fuddle scrambled down a slope and plunged into the forest where he found himself in almost total darkness, for although the day was still bright, the firs and pines cast a gloom so deep it was hard to make out a path.

Fiddle-Fuddle blundered on for an hour or more. Just as he was starting to grow weary and feel hungry again, he tripped and found himself rolling head over heels into a deep pit.

The pit was the den of Greasy Tod, the district's notorious hen-snatcher—the very fox the village women and youngsters had gone to hunt down.

Greasy Tod was just then sitting in a corner of his chamber gnawing on the remains of a fat capon whose feathers lay scattered over the earth. Seeing the Gnome drop into his den, he cut short his feast, made a couple of quick scratches in the earth, swept the bones into the hastily dug hole, covered them over and stared up at the guest. The sight of Fiddle-Fuddle tumbling so unceremoniously into his earth struck him as very funny, but one would never know it by the crafty tod's expression. He lowered his brush modestly and approached the Gnome.

"How now, good sir!" he said sweetly. "Dropping in by the wrong door, I see."

"Indeed," said Fiddle-Fuddle, "it is very dark here, and I seem to have missed the right entrance. Besides, my eyesight has grown weak from my constant labors over my great historical work."

"Ah!" cried out Greasy Tod enthusiastically. "I have the honor of greeting a colleague, a fellow scholar! Why, I, too, spend my life buried in books. I, too, am writing a great work—on the rearing of hens and doves in the villages, to be precise. I'm even proposing a new method of building henhouses. Here are the quills I use for my work!"

And with a modest gesture he pointed to the scattered feathers of the capon he'd recently throttled.

The learned Gnome was greatly amazed. If he himself had won such renown among the Fair Folk with a single quill plucked from a gray goose, then how much greater—he thought—must be the fame of this fellow who'd used up a whole heap of such splendid golden feathers!

Greasy Tod drew nearer to the Gnome.

"And you, dear sir and colleague," he said, eying Fiddle-Fuddle's pen. "How came *you* by such a fine quill? Where would I find the dear bird that fledged it? I'd be very pleased to make her acquaintance."

"The quill came from the wing of a grey goose," replied Fiddle-Fuddle, "one of a flock tended by a little orphan called Mary."

"A flock!" cried Greasy Tod, beside himself with delight. "An orphan girl, you say? A *little* orphan! Doubtless it must be hard for a little girl to mind a whole flock of birds? Oh, how happy I should be to lend her a helping hand. How glad to lighten her load! Know, dear colleague, that I have a kind heart, a very, very tender heart—indeed, soft as Maytime butter!"

And as a sign of the sincerity of these words, he struck his breast with his paw, and drawing right up to Fiddle-Fuddle sniffed the goose-quill a good while.

"Let not my show of emotion surprise you!" he said, wiping his eyes. "I have a sudden sense of my destiny: restoring wayward little goslings to the flock—it is my vocation! Assisting little orphan gooseherds—it is the grand purpose of my life!"

And raising his forepaws he cried out:

"O you innocent little souls! O you sweet, darling creatures! From this day forth I devote myself to your service!"

Saying which he turned and took the learned Fiddle-Fuddle down a long dark passage leading out of his den.

After going a good stretch together, the tod turned to the learned Gnome, saying:

"Do not forget, my dear sir and colleague, to make mention of today's meeting in your illustrious book. Only no high praises, no burning of incense to me! Write simply that you met a great friend of humankind by the name of Greasy Tod—yes, be sure to remember the name!—a great scholar and author of many books; in a word, a fox of an exceptional nature, worthy of every gooseherd's and poultry owner's trust. You understand, dear colleague, natural modesty prevents me from enlarging on my qualities, so I'll settle for a brief mention and leave the rest to your ingenuity."

The fellow scholars shook hands and continued on their way. By now, noticeably warmer air and glimmerings of light were beginning to seep into the passage from above ground. At last, arriving at the spot where the tunnel emerged through a hollow tree-stump, the fox made a sudden leap, and shouting farewell to this comrade vanished into the dense vegetation.

Dizzied by the smell of the damp moss and fresh grass, Fiddle-Fuddle seated himself on last year's fir-cone and rested awhile, overjoyed at having met such a noble animal.

* * *

Fiddle-Fuddle was still sitting on the fir-cone when along came a peasant, axe in hand, a sheepskin jerkin slung unbuttoned over his back, a sackcloth bag over his shoulder, bast shoes on his feet, and a woolen cap on this head—clearly, a village woodcutter. He was making for the forest, gazing up at the sky, evidently in high spirits, for he was whistling to himself.

"Perhaps I should ask this fellow if spring has arrived?" thought Fiddle-Fuddle.

But then puffing himself up with great pride, he said to himself:

"A learned scholar inquiring of a peasant? That would never do."

The woodcutter, glancing aside noticed a fir-cone with some round, swollen object on it. Taking it for a puffball, he brushed it aside with his foot, and went on. Though the woodcutter's shoe barely made contact, it swept Fiddle-Fuddle clean off his feet and sent him and the cone rolling down into a little hollow. Fortunately, the learned Gnome's ink-pot was sturdy and securely corked.

Rolling to a stop in the hollow, Fiddle-Fuddle sat up, felt his bruised ribs, and finding himself in one piece began to grimace and splutter.

"Pish! What a disgusting lout! And I was about to engage him in a conversation! Serves me right! Seems I'll have to go about things differently."

And rubbing his great nose with his finger, he began to ponder the matter. Suddenly, he tapped his forehead and said to himself:

"How am I to know if spring has arrived, if I haven't yet tracked its path around the world!"

And he began looking about for something to use as a globe on which to study spring's course across the earth.

Just then a hedgehog with bristling quills and an apple gripped in his teeth came scurrying by. Delighted to see him, Fiddle-Fuddle greeted him politely and asked if he might borrow his apple. But on spying the strange little manikin, the animal took fright, and having a guilty conscience besides (he'd stolen the apple in the night from a peasant woman's garden and was carrying it to his burrow), he sought his escape. And curling up in a ball away he went rolling down the hill.

"Stop! Stop! Wait!" called Fiddle-Fuddle after him. "I only wanted to trace Spring's path on your apple and give it right back."

But the hedgehog had vanished in the morning mist.

"What a stupid animal!" said Fiddle-Fuddle to himself. "He's made off with that splendid globe of his. What to do now? Look for something else, I suppose."

He resumed his journey, leaping over stones and ruts. Eventually, he found a lump of lime. Shaping it into a ball, he carried it to the top of a nearby hill where, using a fallen pine needle, he began etching out lands, seas, mountains, and rivers; in no time he held the whole world in his hands. Donning his large spectacles, he sat down to study spring's path across the globe.

By now the mist was sinking earthward; for a while, it rippled like a white veil over the valley, enveloping the forest in a light, bluish haze; finally, it rolled down into the hollows to reveal a golden, sunlit landscape of fields, meadows, groves, and oak-stands.

And lo! A beautiful maiden came walking up the southern slope of the hill, her hands raised over the earth, as if she were blessing it. Pansies and daisies sprang up under her feet. Her step was light, her eyes lowered, and all around her you could hear the sound of birdsong and fluttering wings. Her face was dark as fresh-plowed earth, and wherever she passed, rainbows and vivid colors appeared. Bursts of dark-blue light flashed from under her lashes.

It was Spring.

So close did she pass by Fiddle-Fuddle that the hem of her linen garment brushed against him, and the scent of the violet garland binding her flaxen hair wafted past his nostrils. But the learned chronicler, busy with his calculations, failed to notice her. Drawing the sweet scent into his nose, he sat hunched over his great book, diligently writing down everything he deduced from his calculations.

From his calculations he reckoned that spring would not be coming at all. That it had lost its way, got detained overseas, and would not make it to his land. It turned out from his calculations that the larks and swallows would not be singing, for their voices had gone hoarse; that the raucous cawing of the crows would be the only song heard his year; that the winds had blown the flower seeds into bottomless chasms; that neither the rose, nor the lily, nor the crab apple would be blooming. It turned out—this also from his calculations—that dawn had been extinguished; that the sun had dimmed to nothingness; that the days would turn into nights; and that, instead of grasses and corn, eternal snows would be blanketing the fields.

He was writing down these very words, enveloping himself in clouds of smoke from his great pipe, and swelling with pride over his prowess as a sage and prognosticator, when three huge, bristly, golden-black bumblebees, competing in a race through the blue air, came flying over the hill and chose as their goal and finish line Fiddle-Fuddle's bald crown. Once, twice, thrice, they boomed around him, and still buried in his book the scholar heard nothing.

Suddenly, just as he was putting a full-stop to his predictions, *Bam!* something struck his head once—then twice! then again, and again. Fiddle-Fuddle gave out a loud cry; he thought the sky was falling on him. Releasing his pipe from his teeth, he threw down his pen, jumped aside, and in so doing knocked his great ink-pot over his precious book; a black stream flowed all over the freshly written pages. Fiddle-Fuddle froze in horror. So much for his predictions! So much for his calculations! The whole book lay flooded with a river of ink. What would he do now? What would he have to show the Gnomes upon returning to the Grotto? He'd calculated everything so wisely, so beautifully—all for nothing!

The hapless chronicler wrung his hands. The incident caused all his wisdom to desert him; now he had no idea if spring had come or not. And so, in this frozen state he stood until noon, then on into the evening. Stars began to twinkle in the twilight; sweet scents wafted up from the fields and meadows. The beautiful maiden had reached the edge of the forest, and the first maybell sprang up from under her naked foot.

# 2

# Spratkin's Expedition

Meanwhile, the supply of food in the Crystal Grotto had run so low that the daily ration had to be cut to three dry peas per Gnome. Naturally, this led to all sorts of squabbles and even scuffles, which was hardly unusual in times of hunger and cold. Not a day went by but some row or other broke out in the Grotto. Now Maribeetle would have a set-to with Firebrand, now Catkin with Brittlegill, now Puffball with Snowflake; sometimes they'd get into a full-blown brawl, and the grotto guards Muckle and Ruckle would have to lock them up in the jailhouse. But the biggest bellyacher of them all was Spratkin. He ate as much as four Gnomes and was never satisfied.

Now several years before this Spratkin had had a peculiar adventure.

You will recall that not all the Fair Folk fled into the mountains. A good number remained in the villages where they hid during the day under the brick stove or door-sill. Wherever the housewife was careless in her duties, wherever the soup-pot stood uncovered, the dirt remained unswept, the yarn reel was left lying about, wherever the cheese hung not yet fully pressed, the slop pail overflowed, and the chickens went uncounted, then zip! these little pranksters would come out of hiding, drown flies in the soup, sweep the dirt back into the middle of the room, snarl up the yarn in the reel, nibble the cheese, let the hens out of the coop, overturn the slop pail—then zip! dart back under the stove again.

Sometimes, when a woman had a habit of leaving her babe alone in the cradle and running off to gossip with her neighbors, the Gnomes would spirit the child away, replace it with one of themselves, and raise the human child along with their own. Naturally, the changeling didn't grow; only his head grew bigger and heavier, and he'd be so hungry nothing would satisfy him.

Now one such flibbertigibbet had a child named Bartek, a sweet little boy with hair like flax, eyes like cherries, and a mouth like a wild strawberry. A picture of health he was, and happy as a fish in the water. Things would have to be really amiss for him to cry occasionally, and though he was barely six months old, he would smile at his mother, raise his arms and flap them up and down like a little bird.

But the mother rarely spent time with the child; she constantly ran off to prattle with her neighbors. She could neither stand nor sit for long, and when she went out for a round of gossip, she forgot all about her unscrubbed pots, her unwashed laundry—forgot everything, even her little Bartek.

One time, the Gnomes emerged to find the cottage door wide open, the mistress gone, her pigs rooting in the corners, and the boy crying in the cradle. At once they snatched him up, took him underground and, after shaving off Spratkin's beard, placed him in the cradle.

The mother returned home, looked into the crib, looked—looked again! What kind of child was this!—with a head like a full-orbed pumpkin, face all puckered up and wrinkled, eyes popping out, and legs short as a duckling's.

"Saints preserve us!" she cried, rubbing her eyes in disbelief. But then if the changeling didn't yell out: "Eat!"

"Bartek!" cried the mother. "Bartek!" But the child only glowered at her and bawled: "Eat! Eat!"

She nursed and rocked him, thinking he'd go to sleep, but scarcely did she step away from the cradle when he bawled out again: "Eat! Eat!"

This went on into the evening another ten times. The woman could make no sense of it. Whence this insatiable appetite? She put a crust of bread in his one hand, a carrot in the other—and somehow, he fell asleep.

"Did a wolf gaze on you and turn you into a gorger like himself?" mused the woman, marveling at the change wrought upon him. Until now her Bartek had eaten scarcely more than a sparrow; now there was no satisfying him.

Nothing to do but stand by the cradle and give him food, which he gulped down like an old codger, eyes bulging like a frog's—not a bit like her old Bartek!

Several days passed, a week passed. The woman began noticing that whenever she left something in the pot, be it noodles or a mess of peas, and went out of the house, she'd find it scraped clean.

"What is going on?" she wondered, scratching her head.

She thought it was Thomas the cat. So she thrashed him, locked him up in the closet, and went out. When she came back, she found the pot empty, the saucepan licked clean, not a scrap left. She went to the closet, looked in and found Thomas just as she'd left him, his sides sunken in, meowing terribly. Well, if it wasn't the cat then it must be her black housedog Casper. *Then* if she didn't take to the stick! The dog howled in protest. The blows sent shooting pains throughout his body, but the door was closed, no escape.

"Stand still, you little brute!" cried the woman with every swipe of the stick. "A plague on you!"

Casper ran circles around her, jinking and dodging, yelping with pain, and nowhere to hide. Eventually, the woman tired herself out and threw the stick down, and poor Casper, howling pitifully, scampered off to the cowshed with his tail between his legs; and there he licked his aching sides until the evening.

The next day the woman locked the dog and the cat in the closet, set the pots on the stove, and went to her neighbor's. She stayed there a good while, enjoyed a good chat, then came home only to find bedlam raging inside!

The cat and the dog were fighting tooth and nail in the closet—fluffs of fur flying to the ceiling! The cottage stove stood open, the pots were empty, the saucepan was licked clean, as if someone had washed it, and the baby was screaming blue murder in the cradle.

The woman clasped her head in both hands, then banging her fists together in anger, cried:

"Wait, you little mischief! I'll settle with you!"

Awestruck, she approached the cradle, for the little rogue was screaming at the top of his lungs.

The poor woman nursed him, weeping at the sight of her little child. How Bartek had changed! She used to sit with him on the doorstep; passers-by would praise her, saying a sweeter child was never to be found. Now she wouldn't dare show him to the neighbors, such a freak he'd become. He no longer smiled, no longer made pleasant baby sounds or reached for the beads dangling from his mother's neck. Instead, he lay there, bloated and wrinkled—bald as an old gaffer. And grow? Not an inch! Only that head, big and heavy as a pumpkin, making faces at her. A veritable scarecrow!

She tried all kinds of magic on him. She tried tossing three glowing coals and three bread crumbs into a water-bowl; she tried bathing him in an elderberry bath, which was said to ward off the evil eye; she tried fumigating him with willow catkins and scourings from inside the rotted willow-tree that stood at the crossroads. All to no avail.

And now there was the added cost! She was cooking enough to feed two stout peasant lads, but she had so much as to lean out the cottage window then look back and find nothing left in the pot for herself.

"The child is as the child is," said the woman woefully. "The will and the scourge of God! But this guzzling, I won't stand for it! And not knowing what . . . No, I won't stand for it!"

* * *

Next morning the woman boiled a pot of cabbage, another of peas, fried up slices of pork fat, popped it all into the oven, closed the doors, fed the child, and went out, taking the dog and the cat with her.

But she did not go far; she stopped just around the corner and watched through the window. She had not to wait long. Finding himself alone, the changeling suddenly kicked back the coverlet, sat up, climbed down from the crib, and made straight for the oven! He opened the doors, took a delicious sniff of the pork cracklings in the pan, then went looking for a spoon.

The spoons were kept in the spoon drawer. Finding the cupboard hard to reach, he climbed onto a chest, opened the drawer, picked out the largest spoon and went back to the oven, where, taking a hefty helping of cabbage, he dipped it in the fat, added some peas, and wolfed it all down with such gusto that his ears fairly shook.

Terrified, the woman clapped her hands and ran to her neighbor for advice.

In no time the two women came running back to the cottage. They looked and found almost nothing left in the pan, and the little monster, wheezing heavily, still gorging himself silly.

He dispatched the cabbage, ate up all the peas, then scraping the bottom of the pan tipped it sideways, licked up the remaining grease, placed the pan back in the oven, then went rooting about the cottage, peering into all the corners.

The woman clenched her teeth and watched.

Eventually, the mischief found an egg that a hen had laid under a chip basket. He examined it closely, shaking his head in great wonder.

"Seventy-seven years I've been on this earth," he said, "and I never saw a barrel like this—without hoops!"

Right away from these words the neighbor knew it was a Gnome.

"Nothing to do" she said, "but call on God's help, cut down a stout birch switch, thrash the swapling within an inch of his life and toss him on the ash heap. When he starts screaming there, the Gnomes will bring your babe back and take this monster away!"

The advice suited the woman just fine. At once she ran to the nearest birch-tree, broke off a switch, came bursting back into the cottage, and seizing the little rogue by the ear gave him a royal thrashing.

"Take this! . . . This for my food! This for my Bartek! This for my losses! Take *this*! And *this*! And *this*!"

The Gnome screamed to high heaven, but the woman wouldn't let up.

Now there lived two cottages down from her a widow named Puchalina and her little daughter Mary. She had just taken the girl in her arms and was on her way to hoe the squire's fields when, hearing an awful rumpus in her neighbor's house, she stopped.

"Somebody's getting a beating," she said. "We must go and help."

Her little child, who couldn't yet speak, began to whimper, saddened that someone should be suffering such pain and hurt.

The widow looked down the road ahead then at the sun which was climbing higher in the sky. Being a conscientious soul, she was loath to waste time, but compassion got the better of her, and so she went up to the house.

"Neighbor!" she cried, finding the door closed. "Who's that screaming inside?"

"None of your business!" cried the woman. "Go away!"

"Neighbor!" Puchalina cried again. "It's plain you're spanking your little Bartek. Have pity on him, the poor little thing!"

"He's no more mine than an evil wind that blows over the field!" cried the woman.

"Even so," the widow replied, "have mercy! It's painful to hear such screaming!"

And now little Mary began to whimper even more plaintively.

"There's the merciful one!" yelled back the woman. "Such prissy airs she puts on! Go back where you came from and don't poke your nose into other people's business or someone's liable to cut it off—yours and your puling little brat's!"

The angry snub saddened Puchalina, but as things had suddenly quietened down in the house, she said to herself:

"Better let her calm down. People say all sorts of things in anger. No point in taking it to heart. Anyhow, it's quiet now."

And she went on her way.

Meanwhile, the other Gnomes had heard Spratkin's screams.

"Uh-oh! Spratkin's in trouble!" they said. "Nothing for it but go to the rescue."

And wonder of wonders, in less time than it takes to mutter a prayer, a crowd of tiny little folk in green and yellow cloaks appeared from under the stove! Red caps in hand, they bowed low before the woman and begged her to let their comrade go; in return, they'd fill her apron with as many thalers as it could hold.

Hearing the word *thalers*, the woman hesitated, but then her neighbor shouted into her ear:

"Sister, if you believe in God, don't let him go. You'll not get your boy back; and as for the thalers—chicken feed, nothing more!"

The woman heeded her advice.

"Clear out of my house!" she answered the Gnomes. "Give me my boy back, I don't want your thalers! Begone, the lot of you, or you'll get what's coming to you!"

The Gnomes covered their ears; one after the other they darted back under the stove. Meanwhile, the woman, seizing Spratkin by the scruff of his neck, took him outside and tossed him on the ash heap. Spratkin yowled like a tomcat thrown to the ground—as much from fright as from pain, for he had no idea what awaited him there.

Just then Puchalina looked back toward the cottage and saw the poor little creature crying on the ash heap. At once she retraced her steps. She wiped the tears from his eyes, soothed him with tender words, broke off a piece of bread she'd brought for her breakfast, put it in his hand, and pulling up some green grass made a nice dry bed for him. And, since the sun was now high in the sky, she found a large burdock leaf in the ditch and spread it over him like a sun-shade.

Spratkin gazed gratefully at the widow, and seeing little Mary clapping her hands in delight at the sight of him lying so snug on the clean bedding under the burdock leaf, he smiled at her. A great sweetness mixed with great sadness filled his heart.

"May God reward you!" he muttered as Puchalina walked away, child in arms.

The widow would gladly have taken him too, but she didn't dare. After all, he had a mother, and a mother, as everyone knows, though she may scold and even give the child an occasional spanking, will always end up clasping it to her bosom.

So thought Puchalina, not knowing that the Gnomes had swapped the woman's child and that this one was not hers but a changeling.

The day passed. That evening the woman went outside but found no trace of Spratkin. On the doorstep lay little Bartek, quite like his old self, hair like flax, eyes like cherries, and a mouth like a wild strawberry. The Gnomes had restored him to his mother and taken the changeling with them.

Oh, the joy and merry-making that followed! The woman collected a dozen eggs, scrambled them in a pan, and baking a round-cake in the ashes invited her neighbor to celebrate with her.

Now Bartek later grew up to be an obedient boy, but he was always wild. He shunned people, roamed the forests and hills, and told stories of the treasures he'd seen, of the wonders to be found among the Fair Folk living underground. The village held him as a fool and dismissed his tales; and so matters stood for several years.

Meanwhile, Spratkin quickly recovered from his beating. Gnomes know all sorts of herbs and salves with marvelous properties. What with poultices, fumigations, and smearings with oil of nightshade, gnat grease, and spider's bile, they soon healed his stripes.

Now King Glistel loved Spratkin dearly; he doted on him and regarded the eternally hungry Gnome with a kindly eye. Spratkin, in turn, had a great love for the King and often sat at his feet, now warming the royal limbs with his breath, now playing gay tunes on his wooden fife, bringing additional warmth into the Crystal Grotto.

But when it came to food, all Spratkin's thoughts went by the board. Bread was always on his mind. Bowl and spoon in hand, he would push his way to the head of the line and await his ration. If anyone objected, he'd fly into a rage, ready to take on the King's entire entourage.

One day a terrible commotion broke out in the Grotto.

Spratkin became furious over the three dry peas allotted to him by the Court Spencer. Not only did he give the Spencer a sound thrashing, but then he went to the King and complained of the injustice done to him. Alas, the King had to dismiss his complaint. No exceptions to the rule!

Spratkin went to the King and complained of the injustice done to him.

But Spratkin raged all the more:

"If that's how it is, if there's no justice for me here, then I'll go out into the world! I'll find more vittles in any old peasant woman's house than here at the royal table!"

The others laughed at him, saying:

"Go then, you starveling! We'll have one less mouth to feed in these hard times!"

They were joking of course, but Spratkin rejoined:

"Believe me, I'm going!"

Again they laughed at him.

"And bring us back news of spring, if you're so daring!"

To which Spratkin replied:

"See if I don't!"

And girding his traveling cloak around the waist, he thrust his fife under the belt, bowed to the King, and thrusting his tobacco pipe in his mouth made for the exit.

\* \* \*

It was already twilight, when catching his breath at the mouth of the Grotto, Spratkin began to look around. Before him loomed the coniferous forest. Black crows sat cawing in the pines. Unmelted snow still lay in the hollows; wet brown needles covered the ground, and from the dark wall of the eerily soughing trees there blew a damp wind, keen and biting.

"Brr! Winter!" muttered Spratkin; and he looked to his right.

Below him on his right stretched a sparkling valley along which torrents of melted snow from the mountains swept down, unearthing great clumps of fresh sod and feeding the river below. Dusk was deepening over the whole valley.

"Why, that'll be spring!" cried Spratkin, slapping his brow with his hand.

But then an icy blast from the forest blew over him.

"Now let's be wise here!" he said, growing uneasy. "Winter on the left. spring on the right! Which is it? Even King Solomon would have trouble deciding."

Just then a rustling of wings passed over his head.

"Oho!" muttered Spratkin. "Now I'll get to the truth! That's either a raven or a dove. If it's a raven, it's winter, if it's dove, it's spring."

The thought had scarcely crossed his mind when a brown bat swooped down before him.

"Now let's be wise here!" muttered Spratkin again, and he began turning his head to the left and right. Alas, he could arrive at no decision; and he gazed into the valley where everything looked silvery white."

"Oho!" cried Spratkin. "Now I'll get to the truth! Either it's snow or it's dew. If it's snow, it's winter, if it's dew, it's spring."

But on screwing up his eyes and gazing harder, he saw it was neither snow, nor dew, only mist.

"Now let's be wise here!" he growled under his whiskers, growing more unsettled, and he began turning his head to the left and the right, and still he couldn't decide. He looked back at the forest, and there in the undergrowth he spied what looked like a taper-flame of light. "Oho!" he cried." Now I'll get to the truth! That's either a glow-worm or a ghost fungus.[1] If it's a fungus, it's winter, if it's a glow-worm, it's spring." And he ran straight toward the light.

But on reaching the spot, he found himself staring into the eye of a wolf! Spratkin flew into a rage:

"Shine your eye on me, will you? *I'll* shine you a light!"

And saying this he struck a flint, lit his pipe, emitted a cloud of smoke, and turning away ceased to concern himself with the wolf.

Meanwhile, his hunger pangs began gnawing at him with a vengeance. He walked on, seeking something to eat. At last, on mounting the brow of a hill, he spied something lying near a moss-covered rock.

Now this happened to be the very hill on which Fiddle-Fuddle had mapped out the countries of the world, and tried to track the path of spring. On the ground before him lay a round object.

"An egg!" he thought, but it was the globe Fiddle-Fuddle had fashioned out of lime. "A very peculiar kind of egg!" he thought. "Looks like moles have been gnawing at it."

He broke the egg. Dust! That was too much for him, and casting himself on the ground in anger, he pillowed his head on his arm and fell asleep.

It was still a while before daybreak; dawn was barely silvering the eastern sky, when a throbbing sound from above suddenly woke him. Starting up, he rubbed his eyes, looked, and saw a V-shaped formation of storks flying in from the distant

---

1   The *Omphalotus nidiformis*, a gilled mushroom most notable for its bioluminescent properties.

blue sea. All silvery in the spreading whiteness, they swept through the calm air, returning to their ancestral nests.

"Now there would be a stroke of luck!" thought Spratkin. "I'd make better headway on the back of a horse."

And just as he was thinking this, the storks flew directly over the hill on which he was standing and descended lower. Spratkin took a giant leap onto the first stork's back, grabbed hold of its neck, dug in his heels, and leaning forward like a rider giving the horse his head flew off, leading the rest of the flock.

But he'd barely flown over the valley and the river, flashing pink in the dawn light, when he began to notice familiar landmarks: a cattle-track, a pond, field boundary mounds, wild pear-trees, two long rows of huts straddling a village street, a barn, a cow-shed. All these landmarks seemed to stir his memory.

Suddenly he froze in terror. A mist seemed to pass over his eyes. He'd spotted a hut among a stand of birch-trees; in the yard lay an ash-heap stirred up by the hens, and on the doorstep stood a new whiskbroom. He rubbed his eyes, gasping and spluttering. It couldn't be! But there they were, the cottage, the birch-trees, the ash-heap, the broom—all plain as day! Shivers ran up his spine. It was the same hut he'd occupied as a changeling, the same hut whose mistress he'd eaten out of house and home, the same ash-heap she'd thrown him on after his painful thrashing.

"Whoa! Whoa!" cried Spratkin, but the stork, spying its old nest on the ridge cap, broke out into a joyous rattle, and breaking away from the rest of the flock began spiraling down toward the cottage. The poor Gnome clung for dear life to its neck, making himself even smaller than he was.

"Has some evil spell brought me here?" he thought, trembling all over at the memory of the cottage's mistress. He considered making a jump for it rather than risk a second encounter with the woman, but clearly, he'd break his neck from such a leap, and so he clung on.

Meanwhile, the stork described a wide circle over the blackened, moss-covered thatch, then a second smaller circle, then a half-circle, and stretching its long neck and giving out a loud rattle came whiffling down on its old nest. For a moment longer it beat the silent, dark-blue air joyously with its great wings.

Spratkin leaned out from behind the stork's neck and looked down. Everything was just as it had been: a calf bleated in the cowshed, a brown hen clucked, a milk pail hung upside down on the fence post, and old Thomas the cat lay snoring on the doorstep.

Suddenly the door creaked open.

"Horrors! The woman!" muttered Spratkin. The very thought of her made his skin crawl.

"O Storky! Storky!" he heard her calling. "Cheep! Cheep! Cheep! Welcome back, my birdie! Welcome home!"

Spratkin poked up his head then instantly lowered it. Too late!

"What kind of devil is that?" said the woman, and clapping her hands cried out:

"Lawks-a-mercy! Not that same little mischief! What bewitchery is this?!"

And being easily provoked to anger, she cried:

"Just you wait, you little freak! I'll get you with my poker!"

And she ran into the hut to fetch it. Meanwhile, Spratkin leapt off the stork's back, dropped to the bottom of the nest where, burying himself in the straw, he curled up into a ball and sat there, peeking through a crack in the side of the nest.

The woman came dashing out of the hut with her poker and ran her eyes along the ridge of the roof, but all she saw was the red-legged stork standing astride the harrow, happily rattling its bill.

"Where did he get to?" she muttered. "Could I have imagined it?"

Suddenly, a blade of straw tickled Spratkin's nose and he fired off a sneeze, loud as a mortar-shot.

"So! There you are!" she cried, and she tried to reach him with the poker, but the poker was too short.

"Just wait, you wretch!" she yelled. "I'll get me a ladder."

"O, woe is me!" cried Spratkin, frantically looking for a way of escape, his brow breaking out into a cold sweat. Looking down, he saw the woman coming back with a ladder long enough to reach the top of a church steeple. His stomach turned at the sight! Already she'd leaned the ladder against the thatch and was climbing up, poker in hand. The hapless Gnome leapt out of the nest and landed on the edge of the thatch by the smoke-hole.

"Should I jump?" he thought, looking down. Nothing doing! He'd break into little pieces like a painted Easter egg. But the woman was now halfway up the ladder, reaching out with her poker.

"Broken bones be damned," he said. "Anything's better than another beating!"

Already the woman had leaned the ladder against the thatch and was climbing up, poker in hand.

And closing his eyes, he took a run, and leapt. The world spun dizzyingly like a humming-top beneath him: the roof, the woman, cottage and poker all cartwheeled before his eyes. Already he was certain there would be no counting his bones, when he felt himself land on something soft like an eider-down then being instantly borne away at breakneck speed. He grabbed hold so as not to fall off, and even as he did so, a delicious whiff of smoked meat passed under his nose.

It was the woman's cat Thomas! He had just stolen into cottage through the open door, seized a sausage drying by the hearth and was slinking away along the edge of the house when plump! Spratkin landed right on top of him. Feeling something grab hold of his fur and thinking it was the woman catching him in the act, the terrified cat tore off faster than ever. He was already far from the house, the village almost out of sight when, reaching a patch of scrubland, he leapt in and began rolling and tossing about in the thistles and nettles so as to rid himself of the annoying burden. But Spratkin wouldn't let go. The nettles stung him, the thistles scratched him, but so enticing was the smell of the sausage that he was determined nothing should tear him away. Only when Thomas had stopped tossing and released it from his teeth did Spratkin leap off his back; whereupon, seizing the sausage, he wiped the sand off with a burdock leaf, sat down, ate heartily, enjoyed a leisurely smoke of his pipe, then lying down under a bush and musing on his strange adventures drifted off into a delicious sleep.

\* \* \*

Day was slowly breaking; the sun was beginning to shine through the leafage when Spratkin suddenly started and pricked up his ears. Had he heard something? He listened intently. Perhaps he'd dreamed it, as he saw that he was quite alone. But yes, there was a sound in the air! At first, it was like the buzzing of flies, then like the high-pitched whine of gnats; then it became deeper, like a capella of honeybees swarming out into the meadow; finally, the sounds resolved themselves into the strains of the strangest tune, neither loud nor soft, neither a bird's nor a man's, neither sad, nor happy, and yet so poignant that it made you want to laugh and cry at the same time. Spratkin, who liked all kinds of music, listened ever more intently, then observing whence the tune was coming he got up and guided his steps thither. Leaving the scrubland, he entered the pine forest and eventually came out into a glade where a thread of smoke was rising from a campfire; upon it stood a steaming pot that gave off an exquisite aroma.

Drawing these delicious waftings through his nose, Spratkin (being so fond of every kind of food) was about to approach the fire when a nasty little dog having the run of the glade began to growl and bark. A Gypsy lay sprawled on the ground by the fire. He was playing a mouth harp and training a little monkey to dance at the end of a small chain. Hearing the dog bark, he got up and looked around, but he saw nothing untoward. Spratkin, who by this time had a horror of any encounter with human folk, had taken cover behind a sloeberry bush.

The Gypsy lay down again by the fire, and putting the harp to his mouth resumed his training of the monkey. With every twang of the harp he yanked the chain, and the poor creature had to skip now to the left, now to the right; but its movements were so awkward and ungainly that the Gypsy had to keep prodding him with his foot.

"Poor little beast!" thought Spratkin as he watched, for he had a merciful heart; then leaning his head out from behind the bush for a better look he suddenly froze in astonishment. Why, it wasn't a monkey but Fiddle-Fuddle dancing at the end of the chain! Tender compassion flooded his heart, and unable to hold himself back, he made straight toward the fire.

"Can it be you, our learned scholar?" he called out. "Do my eyes deceive me?"

Fiddle-Fuddle recognized him instantly.

"By all that's holy, save me, brother Spratkin!" he cried.

And the two Gnomes fell into a tender embrace and exchanged kisses.

The Gypsy stared agog at them; the harp dropped from his mouth.

"What kind of devilry is this?" he thought, rubbing his eyes in disbelief. "Monkeys not monkeys? Ye gods! They speak with human voices."

Fear seized hm. He almost let go of the chain, but then a new thought crossed his mind, and snatching his hat from his head he clapped it down over the two Gnomes, whereupon, tying up Spratkin with a piece of string, he laughed out loud, saying:

"There! With these two I can make a pretty penny at the bazaar! Monkeys that cry, talk and kiss like people! An opportunity like this comes once in a thousand years if not longer!"

And hastily gobbling down the barley soup he'd cooked on the fire, he got up, smothered the fire with ashes, and with Fiddle-Fuddle gripped in one hand and Spratkin in the other, he strode briskly off in the direction of the market-town.

Poor Fiddle-Fuddle wept bitter tears! He, a learned scholar, having to perform like a monkey at a bazaar!

"Not to worry, learned scholar!" said Spratkin, giving him a gentle nudge. "All is not lost!"

"Oh, dear brother!" groaned Fiddle-Fuddle. "What'll become of my name and renown if I have no book!"

"Why? What happened to it?"

"Gone!"

"And your pen?"

"Broken!"

"Ink-pot?"

"Smashed!"

"Hmm," said Spratkin sadly. "It's true, all your scholarship is lost, since you've no book or pen or ink-pot. But here's what I say: save yourself, but not as a learned scholar but as a simpleton like me! Good shall yet come from this pickle we're in."

He fell silent. Voices could be heard approaching on the road. It was the rest of the Gypsy brotherhood hastening to the town bazaar: swarthy, ragged, kerchiefed women with babes in arm; old crones with clay pipes in their mouths; men with tin pots hanging from the end of a stick; half-naked urchins with wiry hair and sharp, mischievous eyes. The Gypsy joined his companions, and the entire band walked on.

Now our Gypsies would be gypsies! Some stopped passersby to read their fortunes, others snatched up whatever they found unguarded: shawls from the fences, linens from the bleaching tubs, hens from their perches, geese from the meadows, even cheeses hanging from the cottage eaves, drying in the sun. Easy pickings! The inhabitants had deserted their houses and left for the bazaar, and so many other things vanished from the villages along the way. At last, arriving in the town, the band dispersed, some to the right, others to the left; all made their separate ways through the back streets toward the marketplace.

It was a glorious day and the bazaar was abuzz with activity. Scarcely could the square contain the crowd of villagers, horses, cattle and carts! Men gathered around the stalls, trying on shoes and hats; housewives haggled for pots and bowls, girls bought ribbons and beads; children clung to their mothers' skirts, blowing their clay whistles or nibbling on gingerbread cakes. Here and yon, the swaying necks of geese and ducks protruded from openwork baskets. Everywhere there was a hustle, bustle, clucking, quacking, gaggling, and the babble of human voices. But the biggest crush formed around the booth where the Gypsy was standing with his arms on his hips, yelling out at the top of his voice:

"Hurry! Hurry! Step right up! If you've eyes to see, ears to hear, and a penny to spare, come watch the show! Two little monkeys brought straight from the moon! Aye, upon my honor! Straight from the moon! Water they shun, pots they won't wash, man's language they speak, your noses they'll tweak! Step right up! Step right up!"

The people tossed in their pennies and crowded up to the booth where Fiddle-Fuddle was preparing to beat a drum and Spratkin play his fife. Meanwhile, as the people gathered around the booth, the rest of the brotherhood dived in among the peasants' wagons and carts, swiping a sheepskin vest here, a shawl there, a tub of butter, eggs, or a laying hen. But with everybody's gaze fixed on the booth, nobody noticed; only Spratkin saw it. When Fiddle-Fuddle had finished his drum recital, greatly impressing the audience, Spratkin took up his fife, but instead of playing a tune on it, he sang out aloud:

> *Oh fiddle-dee-dee!*
> *Oh, can you not see?*
> *There's thieves in the mart,*
> *Watch out for your cart!*

The people began looking over their shoulders, wondering what could this mean; but Spratkin only repeated:

> *Oh fiddle-dee-dee!*
> *Oh, can you not see?*
> *There's thieves in the mart,*
> *Watch out for your cart!*

Suddenly, a peasant looked into his cart and found his sheepskin vest missing! Another looked to find his recently bought shoes gone! He'd barely come to his senses when a loud cry went up from the womenfolk. The village elder's wife couldn't find her flowered shawl! Then if the people didn't storm the booth and give the showman a royal thrashing! Such a pummeling he got that he let go of the string and the chain; the entire brotherhood cleared out of the town, and in all the pandemonium, Spratkin and Fiddle-Fuddle vanished, as though a gust of wind had swept them away.

\* \* \*

It was late in the afternoon when, arriving breathless at the forest's edge, the two Gnomes flung themselves down on the grass for a rest. Fiddle-Fuddle was especially exhausted, for the chain the showman had attached to his leg chafed against it painfully and made walking difficult. He groaned and hissed in pain, until Spratkin finally broke the chain between two stones then bound up his leg with a wad of fresh grass. Even then Fiddle-Fuddle put up a fuss. Such simple remedies might be good for peasant-folk, he complained, but not for learned scholars. But when at last he felt relief, he settled down.

Meanwhile, Spratkin looked attentively around him.

"Why," he cried out, "this is the same glade where that scoundrel caught me! Hola! If so, there's barley soup to be had!"

And he ran off looking for the smothered fire. In no time he found it, stirred up the ashes, threw on some brushwood and started blowing on it with all his might. The embers began to glow red; sparks flew up from the dry twigs, and before long a bright, lively flame burst forth. Moments later, the delicious soup was bubbling in the pot, and after eating their fill, the two companions lit their pipes and enjoyed a leisurely smoke.

After a while, just as it was time to be moving on, Spratkin's foot knocked against a hard object lying in the grass. Bending down, he found the mouth harp the showman had left behind. Seizing it up, he put it to his teeth and began playing it. Once again that wondrous sound went echoing through the forest; and, suddenly, like a hidden capella awaiting its cue, a throng of thrushes, finches, titmice, whitethroats and other small birds broke forth into joyous caroling. One goldfinch sang so magically that the hawthorn-tree it sat on burst into pink blossoms; pansies and lily bells turned into little winged children and began whispering to each other, "Spring . . . Spring . . . Spring!"

Entranced by the music, Spratkin dropped the harp and leaned forward on his stick. As he sat listening, a plaintive moan—faint at first then growing louder—began to blend with the birdsong and whisperings of the flowers. Presently, a poor, emaciated woman emerged from the forest. She was gathering goosefoot[2] for her meager supper. Wiping the tears from her eyes and thinking herself alone, she crooned in a wistful voice:

> *O, woe! O, woe! O Spring!*
> *O, woe! O, woe is me!*
> *My cupboards are bare,*
> *My Daisy's gone dry,*
> *O, woe! O, woe is me!...*

And forth through forest echoed the woman's lament. Again she sang out:

> *Bare bowls, my tots unfed!*
> *O, woe! O, woe is me!*
> *The fields are a-bloom*
> *Our tables stand bare!*
> *O, woe! O, woe is me!...*

Again, the echoes sprang from tree to tree. And she crooned on:

> *The dewdrops catch the sun,*
> *Yet tears bedim my eyes!*
> *The sun brings the dawn,*
> *And I weep the more!*
> *O, woe! O, woe is me!...*

---

2   Also known as lamb's quarters, wild spinach and fat-hen.

Tender compassion welled up in Spratkin's heart as he sat there listening. He recalled the spring he'd once spent in a poor village when its inhabitants ran out of bread and flour, when mothers had to feed their tots wild forest herbs, when their milk cows went dry for lack of fodder, and the people who had a few grains and husks left for a flapcake counted themselves lucky; and so, when the echoes of the song had faded away, he sighed heavily.

"Now I know it's spring," he said. "The birds are singing, the flowers are blooming, and hungry people weep."

Then recalling that when cast on the ground the sweepings gathered in the Crystal Grotto turned into silver coins, he went quietly up to the spot where the woman was culling her goosefoot, and turning both his pockets inside out began shaking out the contents. And lo! as soon as the dross fell to the ground, it began to glitter brightly.

"A treasure trove!" gasped the woman, seeing the silver coins. "Sweet Jesus! A treasure! So I shan't starve to death! Good-bye misery! Sweet Jesus!"

She gathered up the coins, and falling on her knees broke out into a tender prayer: "You have not deserted us orphans! You have not forgotten us wretched poor, not left us to languish in hunger! Our Provider! Our Comforter! Our Father!"

She fell silent, but the bright tears that streamed from her uplifted eyes continued to speak for her.

The sight of the poor woman brought tears to Spratkin's own eyes, and he broke into sobs. Only after the woman had humbly kissed the ground, risen to her feet, and departed from the glade did Spratkin recover himself and speak out:

"Well, there's no point in staying here any longer! Spring has sprung, and we must get back to the King with the news."

He'd scarcely spoken these words when he heard footsteps approaching on the road; and looking up he saw their tormentor! The disgraced showman had returned for his pot and mouth harp.

Spratkin seized his knotty stick and prepared to defend himself. Fiddle-Fuddle sprang up and was about make off, when his companion grabbed him by the sleeve, saying:

"Have no fear, learned scholar! He played a nasty prank on us; now it's our turn! Doesn't it say in the book that in dire need we Gnomes can turn ourselves back into giants? How do we go about it? Tell me! Quick!"

But Fiddle-Fuddle's teeth were chattering so violently he couldn't get a word out.

"Come on! Out with it!" cried Spratkin, for their tormentor had already reached the glade.

"Y-y-you n-n-need . . " stammered Fiddle-Fuddle, shaking like a leaf, "you n-n-need to name something very b-b-big! The greatest thing there is . . ."

But the showman had already spotted them.

"Ah! There you are, my little birdies!" he roared. "Now you're in for it! Just you wait!"

"Mountain!" cried Spratkin in a shaky voice. But they didn't grow an inch.

"W-w-wisdom!" stammered out Fiddle-Fuddle. But that didn't help either.

"Strength!" yelled Spratkin, now thoroughly frightened, for the showman had laid his hand on him, and still Spratkin remained as small as ever. Then, suddenly, a faint voice fell upon their ears, as though the wind were soughing through the trees.

". . . Mercy!" came the word.

It came from the poor woman returning home through the forest, praising God's mercy.

Scarcely was the word heard when their tormentor paled and froze as though rooted to the spot. The little Gnomes began to grow before his eyes. They grew and grew, and their tormentor drew back.

"Begone, apparition! Vanish! Disappear!" he muttered through lips grown white with fear.

Meanwhile, the Gnomes outgrew him by a head, by two! by three! until standing tall as the forest pines, they towered above him—mighty, massive, menacing! The dwarfed Gypsy cast himself at their feet, and joining his hands cried out:

"Forgive me, your lordships! Forgive me, merciful giants! I thought you were monkeys, but I see you are magicians! Forgive me, I beg you, sirs!"

The giant that was Spratkin bristled his eyebrows and replied in a booming voice:

"Well, perhaps today we're inclined to be merciful! But now you must carry us through the forest and across the river to our Grotto! And gently, mind! Should either of us feel the slightest jolt, or be scratched by a twig, or get our wooden clogs wet, I'll turn you into a mule! And then vittles! you must feed us too. Lots of vittles, good for every occasion! What's that sticking out of your bag?"

It turned out to be a loaf of bread, a smoked sausage, and a wheel of cheese, all stolen from the market.

"Slim pickings! . . . Very slim! . . ." growled Spratkin, removing the foodstuffs from the bag.

But the showman, still prostrate on the ground, cried out:

"Your lordships! Better turn me into a mule right away. How will carry I two giants such as yourselves, and feed you into the bargain? Either way my fate is sealed!"

And he began to whimper and sob. But by now the enchanted word echoing through the forest was fading into nothingness, and the Gnomes began to shrink to their former size. Then Spratkin said:

"Have no fear, Mr. Showman! Rise! You have seen our power and strength! Now we're turning ourselves back into little Gnomes, and you'll have no trouble carrying us. But first we eat! And no skimping, you hear? Feed us as though we were still giants!"

The Gypsy raised his head, and once again found himself facing two tiny little figures. He began kissing their hands, at once laughing and crying; whereupon, setting them on his shoulders, and after feeding them generously and suffering them to light their pipes, he set out on his forced journey.

He carried the Gnomes into the evening and on through the night, for there was a full bright moon in the sky, and though his legs grew weak, he didn't dare complain lest the powerful magicians he'd taken for Gnomes should turn back into giants. Worse still, he received very little of his bread and cheese, for Spratkin kept reaching into the bag and so gorged himself that he swelled up like a pufferfish. So heavy did he become that the Gypsy had to keep shifting the two Gnomes from one shoulder to the other, unable to bear the cramp in his neck that Spratkin was causing him.

Next afternoon they arrived at last at the entrance to the Crystal Grotto. Now the mouth of the Grotto was not wide. A heavy boulder blocked most of it, leaving an opening large enough for any normal-sized Gnome to pass through. As usual, Fiddle-Fuddle had no trouble getting through, as it's well known that learned scholars tend to be thin. But Spratkin had so gorged himself during the journey there was no question of his being able to squeeze through the opening. He tried entering sideways, then turning around tried again—in vain! So he yelled to his former tormentor:

"Hey, showman! Can't you see this boulder has grown bigger and blocks the entrance I used to pass through easily! Move it away!"

But the Gypsy, seeing that his ordeal was almost over, had recovered his courage.

"Generous benefactor!" he said brazenly. "It shall be as you say! But first I'll have my mouth harp back. A Gypsy without a harp is like a bee without honey. I've served your lordships faithfully, so I'm only asking for what's mine."

Spratkin produced the harp.

"Swindler!—he said—Dealer to the end! Now move the rock away this instant, as I've urgent business with the King!"

The stout fellow drew himself up, leaned his shoulders into the rock and pushed with all his might. The boulder lurched heavily then rolled down with a crash into the valley, taking the swindler and his mouth harp down with it.

Day burst into the Grotto in a great flood of warmth and light.

"Greetings, my brothers!" cried Spratkin upon entering.

And several hundred voices answered:

"The sun! The sun! The sun!"

# 3

# King Glistel Leaves the Crystal Grotto

_____

The night was warm and still. Dawn was yet a long way off when, returning home from the market-town, Peter Gelp saw a strange glow by a small rock on the side of the road ahead.

"What's that?" thought Gelp. "A fire that is not a fire? A treasure hoard purifying itself? Do not old folks say that robbers used to live here among these rocks? They buried their gold and silver in the ground, and only a holy fire could purge it of the harm the robberies caused. A hundred years, they say it takes, two hundred in the case of an orphan's groat! Only when the fire has burned out all the harm can such a hoard be retrieved. But only poor folk and orphans can make use of it, otherwise it goes to waste. Oh, if I were that lucky! . . ."

And giving his nag a lash, he drove straight toward the light.

"Will it vanish or not?" he thought as he drew nearer. "If it's not time, it will disappear."

But the light didn't disappear; indeed, the magical irides-cent light around the rock was beginning to shine with greater brilliance, as when a sunbeam is reflected in a dewdrop. The peasant's heart began to beat wildly.

Now Gelp was poor as a church mouse. At home he had two fair-haired little boys whose mother had departed this earth only six months before. These orphans, his wretched hovel, a nag and a wagon were all he had in the world. He scraped out a meager living, hiring out his wagon in the fields, but even so, there wasn't always enough bread in the house. Oh, how he could do with something!—be it a solitary silver coin!

Drawing still nearer, the peasant said a prayer in his heart and imagined how he might buy that strip of land from his neighbor, plant potatoes in it and feed his little waifs. Suddenly, looking closer, he saw in that glow a crowd of little creatures—tiny little folk, barely visible from afar, with long beards, strange clothes, but otherwise quite like little men.

"Gnomes!" muttered Gelp. Shivers ran up his spine, and he tugged on the rein to turn aside, for before such spectacles it is always better to pull off the road.

But the little crowd was already swarming around the wagon, shouting:

"Hey! . . . Hey! . . . Master! Please carry our belongings!"

Before Gelp could say a word, they were climbing all over the wagon. One leapt onto the reach, another attached himself to the wheel spokes, others mounted the tongue, still others grabbed hold of the ladder rungs. A veritable siege!

Gelp pulled up. "What have I stumbled upon?" he thought, looking gloomily and apprehensively about him. But then he felt ashamed that such little folk should cause him alarm . . . What to do now? But there was no time to think, for scarcely had some of these little creatures climbed into the wagon when others began passing up strange caskets and ironed chests from which came bursting that iridescent light; still others were tossing in—as if handling so much clutter—what looked like gold and silver bars,. All these receptacles clanked and jangled and glittered with such luster that Peter almost lost his wits, not knowing if he were dreaming or really seeing these marvels.

Precious stones like rubies, stones speckled like quails' eggs flamed forth from one chest. The air above another shone deep blue from the sapphires inside it—sapphires pure as the limpid sky. A green glow emanating from a casket filled with emeralds lit up all the faces. Here pearls, costly rings there, so seized the eye that you didn't know where to look first. And among all these valuables bustled the sprightly, nimble-footed Gnomes, variegated as a host of tulips blooming in a spring garden bed.

The wagon was almost full, a few last chests and crates remaining to be piled on board, when, suddenly, a wondrous new light, bright as the Morning Star, shone forth. Gelp covered his eyes from the glare, and when he looked again, he saw emerging from a cavern the Gnome King in a purple robe and gold crown; in his hand was a golden scepter mounted with an enormous diamond casting so strong a brilliance that the night became bright as day. Gelp was aghast. Never in his life had he seen such a display of majesty. The only king he'd ever seen was King Herod whose effigy the children carried through the village during the mummers' festival. In his fright he couldn't decide if he should bow before this tiny king or turn around and scoot back down the road. But then the Gnome King waved his scepter benignly, saying:

> *Good evening, gentle wight!*
> *God keep you in his light!*
> *Look sharp, for short's the night!*

And right away, with the help of his lively attendants, the King began climbing into the wagon. Alas, easier thought than done! His purple robe got snagged on a basket, his scepter got hooked on the thwart-bar, the royal crown almost slipped from his head, and his red, gold-embroidered slippers got lost in the hay. The King clambered up as best he could. The greatest obstacle in this proved to be his heavy-footed page Tubkin. Scarcely did the page turn his head when he stepped on the train of the royal robe, then he pulled back too hard on it, then searching for His Majesty's slippers fell flat down on top of him. He got in everyone's way, unwanted as a third wheel. That the King should suffer to keep him around his person bespoke his infinite patience!

Meanwhile, seeing himself in no danger, Gelp recovered from his initial fright. Laughing into his sleeve, he watched the amusing spectacle as he would a Christmas mummers' play. His departed uncle had often told him that Gnomes were the kindest of creatures, and that when they took a shine to a wight, they did him no harm, and even plied him with gifts. Gnomes were only too happy to dwell in kind peoples' homes, biding in mouseholes by day and emerging at night; and when there was work to be done, they helped with the household chores: turning the butter churn, kneading the dough for bread, or spinning yarn on the wheel so deftly that the thread shone like silver. Going out into the yard, they would peek into the stable, braid the horses' manes, or brush them down so that their coats glistened like water. During the harvest season they'd seat themselves on the balk[1] and rock the babe on a bedsheet tied to a willow branch, that it might sleep soundly, and the mother bent over the field with her reaping hook could work undisturbed. If the little child should whimper, they would sing him such lovely songs that when he grew up, these songs came mysteriously to his mind, as if someone had once whispered them to him. Other people would marvel and say, "What a strange boy! He goes about singing and playing his pipe, as if someone had taught him!" But they didn't know that he'd only recalled what the Fair Folk used to sing to him as a babe in bedsheet attached to a branch.

It was the Gnomes, Gelp's uncle had told him, who taught the child to sing. His uncle always made sure to leave them a crust of bread or some farmer's cheese on the bench, since Gnomes would not, of a point of honor, eat off the floor. When Holy Thursday or Good Friday came around, and the household was preparing the blessed food for Holy Saturday, he would break off pieces of this fare, a white round-cake or a smoked sausage, and place them on the edge of the bench for his little helpers. The family holdings grew, and the homestead prospered. Its horses were graceful as hinds, the sheep grew fleece thick as thatch, and the cows yielded more milk than anywhere else in the village, which was not surprising, as

---

1   An unplowed ridge separating one parcel of land from another.

his departed grandmother never failed to leave milk in a walnut shell for the "Poor Folk."

And so things stood for a long time. But then Gelp's grandparents died, and his father after them, and another uncle took the waifs in charge. He quickly put an end to the old order, ran the farm carelessly, neglected the animals, and seized for himself whatever he could lay his hands on. Finally, all was reduced to a condition of wretchedness and want that fairly cried out to heaven. And then it was that people saw the Gnomes emerge from behind the stove, march through the cottage, through the open door, and hence out into the world; and along with them all good things went. The orphans were left with nothing, even as was their uncle who'd sought to enrich himself at their expense.

Such were the thoughts that ran though Peter Gelp's mind as he watched the Gnomes load on the last of the ironed chests and caskets. After finding a fitting seat for their King and covering it with costly velvet, the worthier members of his entourage sat down with him; the rest grabbed hold as best they could, and they all began urging the driver to get underway:

> From shaft to noggin[2] mounts our King,
> So we from shaft to noggin spring,
> Ride forth, ride forth! we Gnome-folk sing!

"Ride? Which way?" asked Gelp resolutely, being now over his initial shock and quite himself. "Right or left?"

---

2   A short horizontal timber member; here, a thwart-bar.

They replied:

> *Rocks to the right, rocks to the left,*
> *Ride straight, straight through the cleft!*

"But where to?" Gelp asked again. Again they replied:

> *Through cornfield, leafy brake,*
> *Across brook, rill, and stream,*
> *For summer digs we make!*

"And what will you pay for the hire of my wagon?" said Gelp, scratching his head.

And they replied:

> *A handsome poppy head,*
> *Purple, white, or red!*

"Out of the question! No deal!" said Gelp firmly. "The horse, the wagon and what's on it are mine!"

To which they replied:

> *The horse, the wagon's yours,*
> *What's on it, ours! Oh woe*
> *To him who'd take what's ours!*

And they drew their swords.

"Then let's go halves!" haggled Gelp. But then King Glistel calmly spoke up:

"My good wight! If you had not a half but a thousandth of a thousandth part of these treasures, it would be to your undoing! Great wealth saps a wight's strength like a disease. A man draws his strength from his native brawn; his spirit he strains through his ribs. A man's strength comes from the good life he leads . . ."

Here the Gnomes broke in:

> *Aye, richlings, moneybags!*
> *They scorn the beggar's rags,*
> *Recoil from sweat and strain,*
> *And though they hoard and gain*
> *They live for naught! . . .*

They fell silent, and King Glistel spoke on:

"Mother Earth did not entrust the bulk of her treasures to you wights, but to us, her little helpers who stand watch over them without material gain for ourselves. We do not turn pearls into beggars' tears. Diamonds we neither buy nor sell. Gold we do not beat into ducats. Enough that the glow of these treasures delight our eyes—that we praise Mother Earth and guard her treasures."

"If His Majesty is so gracious," said the peasant, "then let him tell me where these treasures come from?"

The King replied:

"All these treasures are to be found on this earth, treasures passed up and ignored by human folk. Squandered moments of time turn into sapphires, discarded scraps of bread turn into the shiniest pearls, tiny ounces of strength used not for the good or unselfish gain turn into pure gold. If you wights did not pass up such things, yours they would be. As it is, they go underground, and there we stand guard over them."

"So it's true, you live underground!" said Gelp open-mouthed. "Like blind moles! Dear me!"

"Everything comes from the earth," replied the King. "Small strength, great strength, Mother Earth offers every wight as much as he will take."

"But how do you keep busy there?"

And here again the Gnomes broke in:

> We count the grains of sand,
> The drops that make the stream;
> We count the pearls of dew
> That bead the grass—the sweat
> That beads the toiler's brow!
>
> We count the blooms that grow
> And flourish in the meads,
> We count the forests' leaves;
> We score the birch's bark
> With fanciful designs.

"Argh!" cried Gelp. "An army of flies! How's one to understand them? Your Majesty, bid your subjects sit quiet, as they only confuse a man with all this buzzing. If I'm to drive you, so be it, but I'd dearly like to know where and what for?"

And grasping the reins, he smacked his lips and prepared to drive on, for the wagon was now quite full.

"Drive on in peace, good wight!" said the King, and he waved his scepter. "We shall reward you according to your labor. No harm shall come to you."

"So let it be!" said Gelp. "I take His Majesty at his word! . . . So where are we going?"

The question sent the Gnomes into a tizzy: one said this, another that, and in all the ensuing chatter the King's feeble voice was completely drowned out.

Finally, Fiddle-Fuddle raised his voice, saying:

"Since there can be no kingdom without wisdom, and no wisdom without books in which it stands writ, I propose the good wight take us where there's lots of geese. There I can find a new quill, and build my fame anew."

At this Spratkin, who'd sunk so deep into the hay that only the tip of his nose protruded, sprang up and cried:

"Not on your life! What's wisdom and fame to me if I'm famished? A full belly—that's the main thing! The rest? Worthless as a bag of goat's hair."

And turning to the King, he said:

"Gracious Majesty! If you want peace in your kingdom, see to it first that none should go hungry. Heed my advice: if this wight is to take us, then have him go where there's a hearth, a boiling pot of groats and a skillet sizzling with pork cracklings! Otherwise, no agreement!"

"Aye! Aye!" picked up the others. "No agreement! No peace!"

And there arose in the wagon an uproar such as you hear in the town hall when the councilors are all at loggerheads.

At last, the old King waved his scepter and called them to order.

"If there's no agreement,' he declared, "then hear my command!" And turning to Gelp he said, "Good wight, take us withersoever you wish!"

At this Gelp smiled slyly. Winking with his left eye, and casting a glance at Spratkin with his right, he said to himself:

"Just wait, you tub of lard! The King and the others I'll take where they can fill their bellies. As for you, I've a better place—*Famine Hamlet!* There they'll trim your girth to size . . . See if they don't!"

And lashing his horse he got underway.

# 4

# Spratkin Meets Little Orphan Mary

_____

*Beyond the distant mountains,*
*Beyond three forests deep,*
*There stood a lowly cottage,*
*A cottage called "God's Eye."*

*Why so named? Could it be,*
*Perhaps, because the sky,*
*That gazed down mildly on it*
*Shone clear as God's bright eye?*

*Was it because at Dawn's*
*First flush, ere rose the sun,*
*Its humble thatch stood bathed*
*In God's celestial light?*

*Was it because the brook,*
*That flowed serenely by it*
*Reflected in its depths*
*The azure's brilliant eye?*

*Because the Evenstar*
*That danced above its ridge-pole*
*Gleamed like the tear of ruth*
*Welling in God's kind eye?*

*In weal and woe all night*
*It shone and dimmed at dawn*
*While wights gazed ever up*
*To glimpse God's gracious eye.*

*Be as it may, there stood*
*Beyond the distant mountains*
*Beyond three forests deep*
*A cottage called "God's Eye."*

\* \* \*

*Is it the mourning dove*
*That moans so piteously?*
*The nightingale that pines*
*For springtime's past delights?*

*Is it the forest moaning—*
*The forest dark and deep?*
*Is it the wild wind howling*
*Over the stubbled fields?*

*No dove, no nightingale,*
*No wind, no forest moans;*
*A dying widow weeps!—*
*Laments her daughter's lot.*

*Who'd feed the darling child?*
*Who'd clasp her in her arms?*
*Who'd wipe her cornflower eyes?*
*Who'd take a widow's waif?*

*From sprays and golden reeds*
*She'd woven her a cradle;*
*Dirt floor, the brick stove's shelf*
*Now served her for a bed!*

*With songs she'd lulled her babe,*
*With songs each morn she woke her;*
*Now strangers' rasping voices*
*Would rouse her from the shelf.*

*White cake and golden honey*
*She'd fed her fledgling child;*
*The bitter cake of want*
*Would now be all she'd taste.*

*From whitest woven cloth*
*She'd sewn her little smocks;*
*In tatters now she'd go*
*To graze her little flock.*

*The westering sun sinks down*
*Behind the mountains steep,*
*The mother dies, entrusting*
*Her orphaned girl to God.*

\* \* \*

Poor Mary wept for days,
Whole nights poor Mary sobbed,
But then the larks arrived,
And swallows twittered shrill.

They came one April morn—
A Sunday, bright and mild,
Snowdrops and crocuses
Now decked her mother's grave.

The little girl sat weeping
Beside her mother's grave.
Poor soul! They'd cast her out,
Out of her native home.

Into the world they'd cast her.
Waif, get you hence! Go east
Where peeps the rising sun,
Earn there your daily bread!

Go east where peeps the sun,
Graze other peoples' geese!
The heavy rains shall wash you,
The scorching sun shall dry you.

The heavy rains shall wash you!
Away, you urchin! Hence!
East toward the rising sun!
You've no place here with us!

* * *

Such was the bitter lot of Little Orphan Mary—the sweetest child in the world, with hair like gold, eyes like gentian violets, and a heart filled with sadness and longing.

The mistress whose geese she minded would ask, "Orphan Mary, why do you not smile like other children?"

And Mary would say:

"How can I smile when the wind sighs over the fields."

Or, "Orphan Mary! Why do you not sing as children do?"

And the girl would say, "How can I sing when the birch-trees weep in the groves."

Or, "Orphan Mary! Why do you not laugh and shout as others do?"

And she'd say, "How can I laugh and shout when the earth sheds tears of dew."

Little Mary was that kind of child. And when the birds settling on a tree branch beside her, trilled:

> *Sweet little waif*
> *With golden hair*
> *And eyes so blue!*
> *What do you need?*

She'd look at them sadly and say:

> *I need no silver*
> *I need no gold,*
> *I need a hearth,*
> *A loving home!*

And when the birds sang again:

> *Sweet little waif*
> *With golden hair*
> *And eyes so blue!*
> *What do you need?*

She'd say:

> *I need no bread,*
> *I need no milk,*
> *I need a home*
> *Where flowers grow.*

And turning their heads and fluttering their wings, the birds would chatter among themselves, until one of them trilled:

> *Sweet little waif*
> *With golden hair!*
> *What most you sigh for—*
> *Wish it come true!*

And Mary would raise the hem of her tattered smock with her thin little hands, and showing it to the birds say:

> *Sweet little birds,*
> *You'd have me wish?*
> *To see my mother—*
> *That is my wish!*

Then shortly afterwards her mother would appear to her in a dream. Softly, softly, ever so softly, she'd pass like a moonbeam through the room, shedding her radiance over her sleeping child. Then Mary dreamed the sun was shining, and she could smell the flowers. And reaching out to her mother, she'd whisper in her sleep:

"Mama! Have you come?"

And right above her head spoke a soft, sweet voice:

"Yes, my dear, I have come!"

But these words were like a faint breath.

"Mama, will you take me with you?" she asked, clinging to her mother.

And the voice answered even more softly and sweetly:

> *Now's not the time, be patient, dear!*
> *Who parted us will choose the hour.*

And Mary said:

"Oh, Mama, it's so hard to wait!"

And the voice replied:

> *Work makes the time fly faster, dear,*
> *A day, a life—but fleeting shadows!*

And softly, softly, ever so softly, her mother would glide out of the room, and the orphan would wake with a sigh, rise from the stove shelf, and address herself to her domestic chores. She worked hard for her place on the mistress's stove, worked hard for the handful of straw to strew it with, for the half-ladle of soup she lived on, for the rags that covered her back. In winter she carried faggots from the forest, water from the well; in summer she tended her mistress's geese. And so the people of the village called her Gooseherd Mary or Little Orphan Mary. For a whole year she went so named; then passed another year, until people quite forgot that the girl's family name was Puchalina, and that she was the daughter of that very widow who'd taken pity on Spratkin when the nasty woman beat him for changing places with her little boy. When people asked her for her name, she always answered "Orphan Mary."

The meadow where Orphan Mary grazed her geese stood by a forest not far from a settlement known since ancient times as Famine Hamlet. The land around it was lean and yielded little corn, and more often than not the people there went hungry.

> *Sandy ground, pools of water,*
> *Year of yield, two of hunger!*

Upon this meadow, around these pools, the village raised a great herd of geese. Driven to pasture there, the birds would fight over the meager grass, flap their wings, honk and cackle. You could hear the noise a good mile away.

Grazing the geese was the job of the village children. This they did in groups or alone, as ordered to at home. Only toward the evening would they break up the herd, and each child or group would drive their own flock home. As they passed through the village, all you could hear was the crack of their whips and their cries, "Hah-leh-lah! little geese! Home! Hah-leh-lah! Hah-leh-lah!" You'd swear a wedding party was passing through! And long after sunset the geese could be heard honking in the farmyards and poultry pens. Even at night, a solitary clarion-call would rise up out of nowhere and echo through the district.

But Mary minded her geese alone by the forest. She had only seven birds in her charge, and in obedience to her mistress's wishes did not graze them on the common pasture. She was glad not to, anyway, as her fellow gooseherds made fun of her. The poor child was too slow to play tag or hide-and-seek. Nor did she dance on the grass with the other girls.

And true enough, whether this was because she was too weak living on her meager portion of bread, or simply because she was an orphan, Mary did not like to run or dance or play tag with the children. But singing was her passion! She knew so many ditties she'd sing the livelong day and never run short of them: "Poor Sophy had a yen for nuts," "A grieving pony paws his master's mound," then the ditty about the magic pipe that sang, "Play, dear shepherd, play!" then "Old shaggy Bear matchmaking went," then "Granny had a billy goat," then "O'er the sea the white swans flew." But the song she liked best was the one about the little orphan girl calling to her geese, for it was as if she were singing about herself. When dusk began to settle over the forest, Mary sang out as loud as she could in her thin little voice:

> It's time! It's time, my little birds!
> Alas, time's up for you to graze;
> The night draws near, and I'm afraid,
> I've no one here to walk me home.

A sweet little ditty that went straight to your heart! A passer-by hearing it would stop and shed a tear. No one knew who'd taught her all these songs, and were you to ask her, she'd be at pains to tell you. Had the dark, soughing forest taught her? Had the meadow grasses whispered these songs to her? Had the tender-leaved groves swaying lightly in the breeze murmured a verse or two? Or perhaps it was the silence that stood over the fields and fallow ground, a silence that rang out as though the very air were singing? Little Orphan Mary would listen to these sounds and often forget her hunger and the cold; and when the sun went down and it was time to return to the village, she'd have no idea where the day had gone. Nor would it even cross her mind that hidden in the forest undergrowth, watching her with sharp, cruel and burning eyes, sat Greasy Tod, the sly fox who'd dug an earth for himself under the stump of a fallen pine. There he played the hermit, all the while sniffing out the surroundings for a tasty morsel.

Most of all he craved goose meat. Avoiding the large herd which the strong boys carefully guarded, he set his hopes mainly on the seven geese that Mary watched. And so every day he dug new earths under the bushes, working stealthily toward the very edge of the forest. Meanwhile, Mary grazed her geese, suspecting nothing, then blissfully drove her flock back to the farmyard. Her one helper in this was a little tawny dog called Oscar who'd grown very attached to her. All day long he sat beside her in the meadow.

Now Greasy Tod took a great disliking to Oscar.

"Loathsome little cur!" he'd say to himself, spitting and grimacing. "Never saw a more obnoxious creature! Look at those pointy ears! Entirely unsuited for a dog! And that ginger coat! Why, it's red!—like the traitor Judas. Nasty little beast! What manners! What habits! A regular sponger! No words to describe how much that animal disgusts me. The very sight of him makes me sick. Whoever saw a real dog sit all day long in one place guarding seven wretched geese? Has he no shame? Seven measly geese! Ha, ha, ha! . . . Makes one want to laugh! Show me the meat-loving simpleton who'd go for such meager pickings? In the old days, perhaps, it was common for a plump goose to grace a fox's table, for it is well known that our elders had their peculiar ways. But the abstemious fox today doesn't hanker after such delicacies! I, for one, am not partial to goose meat. Nor can I bear the sight of that yellow dog and that little tattercoat of a girl. If I hadn't the intention of being a hermit, I'd long since have moved out of this district. But then, when someone devotes himself to a hermit's life and penitential living . . ."

Here he'd sigh so mightily that his whiskers would curl around his nose, and winking first with one eye then the other, he'd follow every movement the dog, the geese, and the little girl made. And so for a good while he'd sit watching; at last, he'd turn and slink back to his earth, a cruel smile spread along his pointed snout.

\* \* \*

Famine Hamlet was already growing visible in the moonlight. Peter Gelp was heading toward it, having taken a detour from the highroad. Suddenly, he turned to the Gnomes in the wagon:

"My simple mind," he said, "tells me I shouldn't drop all your honors off at once. If this many mouths were to descend on one village, the cost would be steep. Some might even end up going hungry."

"Right!" answered a resolute voice from deep inside the wagon. It was Spratkin buried up to his ears in the hay. "Drop us off in twos, threes, or fives! It'll be easier for the housewives, and the rest of the villagers, too!"

"Prudent observation!" said the King. "Let it be as you say."

Gelp halted the wagon, and pointed to the nearby hamlet.

"So it's to be two or three at this village, is it?" he said, scratching his head. "Oh, they'll be sitting pretty here, for this is Fat City, the richest settlement in the district! Every peasant is his own master, and all those pastured here weigh as much as an ox. The women and children trundle about like barrels—that's how round and fat they are! And why wouldn't they be when all they do from morning to night is kill, cook, baste, and salt, as though Easter came every day? First thing in the morning a peasant sits down before a bowl and won't budge from the table till noon, so as not to have sit down for the next . . ."

"Stop! Stop!" cried Spratkin from under the hay. But Peter lashed his nag and drove on past the village as though he hadn't heard him.

"And why wouldn't he sit there from one bowl to the next," he went on, "when the fields practically sow themselves? And oh! Did I mention the bacon, the pork cracklings, the goose fat? A bottomless supply! . . ."

"Stop! Stop, I say!" cried Spratkin louder, thrashing about in the hay. "Stop, when I tell you!"

"Eh, what's that?" said the peasant, as though he'd just heard him.

"You're not pulling our leg are you, peasant?" said Spratkin, digging himself out of the hay and looking at him sharply in the eye.

"Why should I be pulling your leg? Cross my heart it's true!"

"Lots of grub, you say?"

"As much as the belly will hold!"

"Lots of sauce?"

"So much it drips down your beard!"

"And the bowls, are they big ones?"

"Big as the moon up yonder!"

And after looking up at the moon that hung low over the horizon, Spratkin turned to the King:

"That's it then! This is where I get off."

And squeezing the King's knee then bidding his companions on the thwart-bar goodbye, he called to the driver to turn back. Gelp, who was only too happy to oblige, turned rather too sharply; in so doing, he ran over a rock: the wagon lurched, jolted upward, and Spratkin shot out of the wagon, described a graceful arc in the air and found himself lying on the ground. Fortunately, he was not harmed, for the sand he fell on was soft as an eiderdown. Nevertheless, he let out such yowl that he woke every dog in the village. Their noise woke a gander, then another; a watchful goose picked up the alarm, then another, then ten, then twenty, whereupon there arose in the farmyards and poultry pens such a tremendous clamor you'd think the whole village were on fire.

"My bones! My aching bones!" yelled Spratkin, feeling his ribs, terrified by all this honking and gaggling, but he was barely heard in the noise. Meanwhile, the driver stung the nag's haunches with his switch and headed off at a fast gallop.

Spratkin rose to his feet and looked around him. Suddenly, he became aware of someone scratching about in the sand beside him, and when the moon peeped from behind a cloud, he saw to his great surprise that it was Fiddle-Fuddle.

"Do my eyes deceive me?" he said. "Can it be you, our learned scholar?"

"Yes, it's me!" said Fiddle-Fuddle.

"Don't tell me you fell out of the wagon too?"

"Why, no!" said Fiddle-Fuddle. "I jumped out with the King's permission. You see, dear brother, all this gaggling can only mean one thing: that there are geese around. Do you follow?"

"As day follows night."

"And if there are geese around, there must be feathers, right?"

"You don't say!"

"Why, yes! It's clear as two time two makes four, right?" continued Fiddle-Fuddle. "And if there are quills here, then my glory lives, since I shall be able write a new book to replace the old one. Do you follow?"

"As the tortoise the hare," said Spratkin fervently.

But though he assented warmly to everything his companion said, Spratkin wasn't pleased at the prospect of having to share all those delicacies he'd promised himself.

"Know what, learned scholar?" he said after a pause. "In my opinion, it wouldn't do for a sage like you to barge in on the peasantry and sit down to a bowl with these simpletons; it might dull your keen intellect. So here's what I propose. I'll go into the village, and you go into the forest. At night when everyone's asleep I'll bring over a bowl and you can have whatever's left in it. I know, I know . . . you've sometimes got the short end of the stick, but that's all right. Remember one doesn't live on bread alone. At least you'll have upheld your honor. And honor's the main thing!"

"Good advice, dear brother!" said Fiddle-Fuddle wistfully, and throwing his arms around Spratkin's neck he hugged and kissed him.

The gesture saddened Spratkin, for at bottom he had an honest heart. He felt a pang of guilt that his underhanded advice should be so readily accepted, but since the voice of his greed was stronger than his heart's, he quickly shook off his sadness, and hugging Fiddle-Fuddle back accompanied him to the forest; whereupon, after bidding him good-bye and wishing him the wisest of thoughts, he crept along the fences and directed his steps toward the largest cottage.

Alas! Never in his life did he meet with greater disappointment! The cottage pantry was so bare a mouse would have starved in it. The kneading trough stood plastered with dry husks and chaff. Not a pork crackling, not a grain of groats, not a whiff of sauce or goose meat. Spratkin looked into the pots—all empty, and no sign that anything had been cooked in them the day before. He looked into the saucepans—same thing! He left the cottage, ran to the next, then the next, but none fared any better. He looked into the fifth, the tenth—All bare and empty! And the people sleeping in them, all skin and bone! No decent sheets, no cooking pans worthy of the name, not even a good horse in the stable or a cow in the cow-shed. Many of the hovels' roofs sagged pitifully and had to be held up by poles, like cripples on crutches. Even the village elder's house fared no better! Such was the springtime scarcity of the village.

"Why, that cunning peasant!" cried Spratkin furiously, clenching his fists. "He played me for a fool! So it's abject poverty I've fallen upon! I've been tricked! And he called it Fat City! 'So much it'll drip down your beard!' he says. 'As much as a belly will hold!' So here's your grub! Your sauce! And now I'm left standing here to dry out like a fence post. If I could just have a crumb of bread. A teeny slice of sausage! A tablespoon of soup!"

Day was breaking and the wretchedness of the village was becoming increasingly more apparent when Spratkin, standing at the crossroads, raised his head and began to read the sign nailed to the post. He read it and read it, and couldn't believe his eyes! Was he seeing things? He read it again: Fa-mine Ha-m-let. It couldn't be clearer: Fa-mine! Spratkin wrung his hands and stood there, plunged in the deepest despair; meanwhile, the sun was slowly rising from behind the forest.

Once again, he looked sadly at the sign: Famine Hamlet it read, clear as day, and he let out a heavy sigh.

* * *

Meanwhile, Fiddle-Fuddle, who had been pacing all night long in the forest, slapping his sides to keep warm, happened upon a great mound of sand beside a deep burrow. A single glance at it would have told him it was a fox's earth, but having spent his entire life buried in books our chronicler knew little about such things.

"A mountain? Not a mountain?" he wondered, stopping in his tracks. "A stronghold? Not a stronghold? Hmm, who knows if this isn't one of our ancestors' ancient temples? Entirely possible! Entirely possible!"

And very carefully he began to circle the mound. Suddenly, a red, triangular head with burning eyes and uncommonly strong sharp teeth poked out of the burrow. Out it came, then immediately drew back. Seconds later, it poked up again, and this time the full length of Greasy Tod's sleek body emerged with it. The fox recognized Fiddle-Fuddle at once but pretended not to know him.

"And who might this strange wayfarer be?" he said in a grave, dispassionate manner. "What seek you in these precincts devoted to serious study and penitential living?"

"I am the court chronicler of King Glistel of the Crystal Grotto at your service, Your Excellency," said Fiddle-Fuddle politely.

"Why, it's you, my learned scholar!" cried Greasy Tod. "What happy chance brings you here? What? Don't you remember me? Forgotten already? Why, I'm Tod, the learned author of many books whom you were so kind to drop in on some time ago."

"Why, of course!" said Fiddle-Fuddle, slapping his forehead with his hand. "I do remember! As if for a moment I could forget! Please forgive me, Your Excellency."

He said Your Excellency because it didn't seem right to address such a noble animal by the title Sir, as one would the best barber in town.

They fell into each other's arms, kissing each other in turn. Then Fiddle-Fuddle inquired of the fox:

"I wonder if Your Excellency wouldn't mind explaining the significance of this mound I see here before me? I hope you don't think me too forward for asking?"

"Not at all!" said Tod with a laugh. "I had this sand brought here so as to have enough on hand to cover my learned books with!"

Here he lowered his gaze as if deep in thought, and wiping his brow with his forepaw added humbly:

"I worked very hard on them . . . very hard. But tell me," he said with renewed animation, "how goes my learned friend's book?"

"Ah!" groaned Fiddle-Fuddle, "Better not talk about it! I met with the worst misfortune that can befall an author. My book was destroyed and I broke my pen!"

"Your pen! Broken?" exclaimed the fox, and the eyes in his head gleamed, and his teeth seemed to grow sharper.

"Why! Nothing easier than to get another, and not just one! Five, ten! What am I saying? I'm ready to supply my learned friend with a hundred quills—in return for one teeny-weeny favor, a favor as tiny as a grain of sand! This very day! Soon! In an hour."

And taking Fiddle-Fuddle by the arm, he led him back and forth, confiding in him in a collegial manner.

"You see, my friend, there's a dog in the neighborhood I simply cannot abide. Why exactly, I don't know—perhaps it's his ugly exterior or disgusting habits. Anyway, he spends whole days idly guarding seven wretched geese that stand in absolutely no danger. Enough that I cannot stand the sight of the beastly thing and should be glad to be rid of it, even for a moment or two. As if to spite me, the creature comes every day to the forest's edge along with a little tattercoat of a girl and her scrawny geese and sits right by my den, poisoning my hours of learned study with its presence. Now, dear friend, as soon as he arrives today, I want you to lure him away for a while, that he may leave me in peace to finish the labor I've long been busy with. If you'll accomplish this task, I promise you a whole handful of the choicest quills, with this special added virtue that when you take one in your hand, you'll go to sleep in the evening, and when you wake up in the morning, you'll have a quarter of your book already written. Now how's that for a quill!"

Fiddle-Fuddle swallowed hard, and his eyes lit up.

"Why, no trouble, no trouble at all!" he said. "With all my heart! Whatever Your Excellency deems fit! I'm at Your Excellency's service."

And he bowed to the fox, and swaying to the right and left he grasped both his forepaws with great sincerity.

\* \* \*

Meanwhile, the morning mist was melting away to reveal a clear blue sky above. Ganders honked, geese gaggled; here and there, a cockerel crowed. Before long, the whole village was a-stir: well-sweeps creaked, cattle lowed, and wisps of bluish smoke were rising above the thatched roofs, a sign that the housewife had shaken out what was left of last year's flour and was cooking soup for the cottage inmates. She boiled the water, mixed in the flour, added a little whey, salted it, and poured it into the bowls, shouting:

"Quickly, children, come and eat! Natalia, here's your spoon! Hurry, Amelia, before Nathan eats it all! Come on! Come on! Two spoons, down the hatch! That's it! Quick, before the sun dries the pasture."

Soon you could hear the cruel crack of the whips and the shrill cries of the children: "Hah-leh-lah, little geese! Hah-leh-lah! . . . Hah-leh-lah! . . . To pasture! To pasture!" The sandy road swirled, the cries of the geese mingled with the children's yells; whip-cracks rent the air, and overtopping this noise rose the terrible cry of the elder gander who flapped his wings and strutted before the herd like a commander leading his army.

But from one the homesteads hastened a very small flock of geese consisting of just four white and three brindled birds. Padding behind them, in a threadbare blouse and dark-blue skirt, came Little Orphan Mary. Her clothes were clean, her golden hair was braided, and her face was beautifully washed. So lightly did her bare feet tread the grass that the blades scarcely felt her weight. Beside her ran her little tawny dog, wagging his tail and barking whenever a goose strayed from the herd. With such a good helper Mary needed no whip for her flock. She carried only a willow branch; and with this little branch, she skipped over the white dew, singing sweetly:

> *Where stands her keeper's house*
> *An orphan toiled and moiled,*
> *But dawn's gold light would help her!*
> *For scraps of bread she toiled,*
> *The bright sun helped her, too!*
> *Hah-leh-lah! Hah-leh-lah!*

So singing, Mary arrived at the meadow. There she seated herself on a knoll, and the gaggling geese fell to grazing about her, nibbling on the early morning grass. Her faithful dog Oscar ran around them once, then twice, now nipping a brindled goose for straying too far, now yapping at the white gander for not minding his flock; then lying down at the meadow's edge, he watched the forest.

Now Oscar was a very sensitive little dog! The forest's outermost trees leaned over his little mistress, whispering mysterious words, as though assuring her of their protection. On the side opposite where a narrow cornfield ran wedge-like into the pasture, the grain-spikes bowed, now toward the forest, now away from it, now listening to the forest's whisperings and gleaning various snippets of news, now passing them on to their fellows who stood out of hearing range. Beetles, bees, gnats joined in these murmurings, spreading the news in their own way, now droning, now humming softly.

Only the tawny hamster turned a deaf ear to these murmurings. He lived in a small burrow on the nearby balk, and every day he worked diligently, laying up his food stores ahead of the harsh winter to come. Only when his little jaws grew numb from gnawing on the grass and ears of grain, and his back grew stiff from carrying the straw and seeds into its burrow—only then would the thrifty little animal straighten his back, rear on his hind legs, and with his little black eyes darting now to the left, now to the right, begin noticing things around him.

The hamster was used to the sight of the yellow dog and the white and brindled geese. He hated the dreadful noise they made, but he loved to hear Mary sing. Her songs so went to his heart that she had only to strike one up and he would drop his labors, rear on his hind legs, pivot his head, twitch his little whiskers, and whistle softly, as though he were accompanying her. Mary saw the little animal, and as her singing seemed to give it such pleasure, she sang to amuse it as well.

"The little thing's alone in the world, just like me," she said to herself. "He, too, must be sad at times. Perhaps this song will cheer him up a bit." And she sang out in her thin little voice:

> *Old Shaggy Bear matchmaking went,*
> *With ale he went to She-Wolf's den;*
> *That spring Old Gray Wolf She-Wolf wed,*
> *Ne'er had the guests a richer spread!*

As soon as the hamster saw that the smiling girl was singing for his amusement, he reared up, twitched his whiskers, turned his head, and whistled softly. Mary had long wished to befriend him, but the animal was so wild that every time she approached him, he'd drop back onto his forepaws and vanish into the grain, so that only the stalks and ears stirred behind him like running water when you throw a stone into the stream. So she left him to his wild ways.

Oscar also watched the hamster, but he only said to himself:

"Why chase after this brash little whistler that stands on two paws and pretends to bark like a watchdog? Must be some comedian, as even its whistling's a pretense! Don't the village boys whistle like that, only louder? Even its whiskers aren't real, since, I ask you, whoever saw whiskers on such a wretched creature pretending to be a cat? Why, it doesn't even compare to a cat! Best thing is to turn away from it."

And he turned away so that all the hamster saw of him was his bushy tail. Even so, as Oscar lay curled up in a ball, dozing, he would open one eye, then the other, and cast a glance at the little animal. Now and then he growled softly, as though he'd dreamed something unpleasant. But being a proud and resolute dog, and having decided to leave the hamster be, he made no advances toward him. Besides, wasn't he busy enough with the geese? Driving them away from the cornfield, keeping them from the forest, making sure every moment the tally was right: four white and three brindled birds. Why, with all this, you needed a mind like a high court!

Suddenly, ever alert to his surroundings, the hamster spied the triangular head of a fox—a stranger in the woods—poking out of a clump of hazel bushes at the forest's edge. Right away he realized the fox was stalking the little flock grazing on the meadow knoll. Twitching his whiskers, he began to debate with himself:

"Should I warn them? It would be easy to do so! Perhaps I should? There's evil intent in those eyes, and look at that snout? A roguish one if ever I saw one! Only I'd have to scramble up that hill, and that doesn't appeal to me at all. Not in this heat! Besides, the field mice or other rodents might make off with some of the grain I've so laboriously cut down. After all it is *my* hard work! Ekh! . . . Each to his own labors! Anyway, the girl's just sitting there. If she has time to sing, then she has time to watch her geese. She sings nicely because she sings, that's all! But duty before singing. That's what she's here for, to mind the geese . . . And the dog? What's he sitting idle for? If he can growl and turn his back on me, then he should be able see the fox in the bushes. Is it my job to mind someone's geese?

And what reward would I get? A mere 'thank you' cackled by a goose or two? What a joke!"

Here he whistled and laughed, and flashing his black eyes dropped back on his forepaws and resumed gnawing on the ears at the edge of the cornfield.

Now my readers should know that although hamsters are natural farmers, they tend to be selfish. Apart from the field, the work they put into it, and the profit they gain from it, nothing else interests them. Hamsters care only for themselves.

Mary watched the animal at his labors. What pleasure it gave her to see him—*her* little hamster, she called him—drag his winter stores from the field, cram them into his burrow then pop out again and return to the field for more supplies! When he disappeared into the corn, she turned her attention to her geese and ran her eyes over the meadow. Her gaze fell on the yellow flowers growing thick as stars all around her.

The air was terribly close, the hot sun was beating down, and Oscar, tongue hanging out of his mouth, panted loudly. Sweat broke out on the Mary's brow, but she didn't seem to notice. She was weaving a garland for herself and happily singing:

> *Where stands her keeper's field*
> *An orphan toiled and moiled,*
> *But the field flowers helped her!*
> *Her keeper's geese she grazed,*
> *Sweet Jesus, too, would help her!*
> *Hah-leh-lah! Hah-leh-lah!*

Suddenly, Oscar barked once, then twice. Something had stirred in a hazel bush at the edge of the forest. For a moment the leaves rustled softly then fell still. Raising himself on his forepaws, Oscar pricked up his ears and listened. Once again he heard the rustling, then silence again. He growled and bared his teeth.

But Mary did not hear him. As a bird sits warbling on a branch in the grove and fails to hear a cat creeping toward it, so the little orphan, seeing nothing, hearing only the sound of her own sweet voice, sang blissfully on:

> *The orphan lived with strangers,*
> *On strangers' fields she toiled,*
> *And sweet Lord Jesus helped her!*
> *The sun, the flowers helped her,*
> *But Jesus helped her more!*
> *Hah-leh-lah! Hah-leh-lah!*

Just then the strangest little figure leaned out from behind a hazel bush—a tiny homunculus in a red cap and traveling cloak, with a white beard, and a pair of spectacles perched on a prodigious nose. Instantly, Oscar sprang up and made for the bush, but even before he reached it, the little figure was leaning out from another, wagging his finger. Oscar tore off after him there, but now the little hooded figure was peeking out from yet another shrub. The faster the dog raced toward the forest, the faster the red hood darted among the bushes, dodging to the left and right. Soon they were deep inside the forest among the tall pines. Just as Oscar was beginning to gain on his quarry, the little figure darted aside and scrambled up a tree, whence, reaching the top, he looked down over the top of his spectacles and began wagging his finger at him. Enraged,

Oscar leapt at the tree, barking so loudly that he roused his mistress from her song. Hearing her faithful helper's furious barking, Mary began calling out in great terror, "Oscar! Oscar!" And scrambling down the knoll she ran into the forest.

Here was the moment Tod was waiting for. With a single bound he fell upon the geese, seized the nearest one by the throat and throttled it before it could cry out, "Help!" Casting it like a rag doll into the bushes, he seized the next bird, sank his sharp fangs into its neck and shook it with such violence that it gave up the ghost before it got halfway through a cry.

Seeing her slaughtered geese, Mary gave out a terrible cry.

Tossing it, too, into the bushes, he fell upon the rest of the flock. The geese, seeing the marauder, raised an appalling cry and fled in a deadly rush before him, some sprinting toward the cornfield, others taking to wing. But with one leap Greasy Tod pounced on the most beautiful brindled goose, snapped his jaws once, cast her to the ground, then went after the others. Unable to remain in the air for long, they were falling with dreadful screams to the ground before his very jaws. Mary heard their screams, and crying out with an inhuman voice ran breathlessly back to the meadow. But by now Greasy Tod had dispatched the last of the seven geese and was licking his bloody chops, surveying his killing ground with burning eyes.

As though borne on the wind, Mary flew back out of the forest; as though borne on the wind, she burst out upon the meadow, and there, seeing her slaughtered geese, she let out a terrible cry: "O Jesu!" and she fell senseless to the ground.

* * *

Anyone walking by the forest early that morning would have been amused by a most comical sight. A tiny little figure in a red cap and cloak was executing strange leaps in the boggy ground adjacent to the forest. From clump to clump it sprang, now grabbing hold of the sharp-edged reeds, now breasting the grass like a swimmer, now sinking deep into the mossy bog.

It was none other than our friend Spratkin. But how he'd slimmed! Of his former flab there remained as much as you'd find on a gnat. His cloak looked as if it had been borrowed, so

loose did it hang on his back; his little legs, which kept parting company with his clogs, stuck out like matchsticks; his
huge head swayed on an excessively thin neck, and his poker-
thin arms could scarcely bear the weight of his tobacco pipe,
which was packed not with shag but alder leaves! Such was
the change Famine Hamlet had wrought upon our stout little
friend. And there were other changes as well.

The hunger Spratkin had recently endured had taught
him many things. It taught him to leap from clump to clump
while roaming the bogs in search of peewits' eggs. "Pee-wee!
Pee-wee! Pee-wee! Pee-wee!" cried the bird, beating her
wings over the Gnome's bobbing head. Poor little thing! She
thought her shrill cries would scare off the invader who at any
moment might stumble on her nest in the grass and plunder
that first single egg she'd laid this year. When the bird kept crying louder and louder, almost deafening the Gnome with her
screams and beating wings, Spratkin stopped.

"Stop your squawking, you silly bird!" he snapped. "What
are you, a magpie? You think I wade in this quaking bog for
pleasure? I've still sense enough to prefer a piece of sausage to
your egg! I do it out of hunger—hunger that would deprive
me of my life! So leave off! Don't wag your beak at me, or I'll
wring your neck!" Then lowering and shaking his head, he
muttered to himself sadly: "Dear God! What a predicament
I find myself in, and who knows what's to come yet! O that
cursed Gelp! I reckoned on Fat City, not Famine Hamlet!
Curse the scurvy peasant for bringing me to such straits!"

Just as he was saying this, he heard what sounded like bitter
sobbing. Drawing back his hood, he hollowed his hand and

put it to his ear. Yes! Clearly someone was crying; it was the voice of a child.

"Heavens!" said Spratkin, for deep down he had a compassionate heart and was easily moved by other creatures' misfortunes. "Heavens, if the poor thing isn't in a worse predicament than I! I'll go and see what's the matter!"

And forgetting all about his hunger, and to the great relief of the bird, he turned toward the forest, guiding his steps by the sound of the voice.

"Yes, clearly a child crying!" he said, stepping stork-like from clump to clump with ever greater strides. Emerging at last from a thick clump of bulrushes, he spied a little meadow at the very edge of the forest. There, on a knoll, sat a little girl. She had both hands over her face and was sobbing bitterly. Deeply moved by the sight, the Gnome hastened toward her.

"Why are you crying, my little lady?" he said upon reaching her. "What misfortune has befallen you?"

Mary started, and withdrawing her hands from her face gazed wide-eyed at Spratkin, speechless from shock. So Spratkin spoke again:

"Please, don't be afraid, little miss. I wish you no harm. I am a friend!"

"Sweet Jesus!" whispered Mary. "What am I seeing? A creature, small as a doll, yet it talks like a man! Jesu! . . . I'm afraid!"

And springing up from the knoll, she tried to run away, her arms raised like a bird about to take wing. But Spratkin blocked her path, saying:

"Don't run away, little lady! I am Spratkin the Gnome, and I wish to help you!"

"A Gnome!" said Mary, as if to herself. "Why, of course! Mama used to tell me about Gnomes, and how good they were."

"Your mother speaks the honest truth," said Spratkin unabashedly, "and I'd be happy to thank her for it."

Mary shook her golden head.

"My mother's dead! . . ."

"Dead?" said Spratkin. "Oh, what a grave word! Heavier than a stone!" And shaking his head, he sighed.

"What was your mother's name?" he asked.

"Puchalina!"

"Puchalina? . . . Why, we've met! You're the little Mary that shed silver tears of pity when that nasty woman almost beat me to death. Ah, my benefactress! My queen! So we meet again! Fortune unites us once more! O speak! Tell me how I may cheer you in your great distress."

"No, no!" she said, sobbing. "Nothing will cheer me!"

Spratkin came right up to the girl, and hiding his pipe behind his back began to console her with sweet words.

"My little lady, do not mar those dark-blue eyes with such bitter sobbing!"

"I'm not a lady. I'm Little Orphan Mary!"

"Then all the more would I serve my little lady! I beg you, enough of these tears! Where is your home?"

"I have no home!" she said. "The mistress whose geese I minded threw me out."

"Ah, the nasty, wicked woman!"

"No, no!" countered Mary. "I'm the wicked one! It's my fault the fox killed the geese. My dear geese! My precious little geese!"

And again she covered her face and burst into sobs.

"Come now!" said Spratkin, removing her hands from her face. "What good is all this crying? You must go back home!"

"No, no!" wailed Mary all the more bitterly. "I cannot go back! I shan't! I'll go out into the world. Into the forest! Go where my eyes lead me!"

"But what would you do in the forest? The world's no kitchen garden you can circle in a moment. Why punish yourself so?"

The Gnome began to pull and nibble at his silver whiskers.

"Perhaps I could help you repay your mistress for the lost geese?" he added after a pause. "Was there a lot of them?"

But Mary only sobbed the louder. "What good would that do if they're all dead!" she cried. "Throttled! Mauled to death! O Jesu! Jesu!"

Seeing the little girl's deep and inconsolable grief, Spratkin bent his head in thought and began tugging on his whiskers again.

"If that's the case," he said at last, "then there's nothing to do but go to the Queen of the Southern Mountains. She alone can help us!"

At once Mary raised her eyes. Like two dark-blue stars they gleamed with renewed hope.

"But is she a good queen?"

"I see you have prudence beyond your years," said Spratkin, "since you ask first if she is good and not if she is powerful. For, what is power without goodness? Nothing! Less than nothing! And since you give me courage with your good sense, why don't we make the journey together, as it's a long and arduous one! I'll gladly take you to the Queen of the Southern

Mountains. An orphan's tears cry for redress and all manner of assistance."

Hearing these words, Mary wiped her eyes and said, simply: "So, shall we go?" And off they went.

# 5

# Good Times

————————

"Where is this wight taking us?" the Gnomes asked one another as they sat on the poor peasant's wagon thinking about their two comrades Spratkin and Fiddle-Fuddle who'd vanished on the way.

"Some king's palace, I imagine," said Chancellor Sharpeye, "somewhere where His Majesty will find suitable company and suffer no slight to his honor."

"Oh, wouldn't that be grand!" piped up the page Tubkin, and licking his lips liberally he added: "I hear kings dine only on the richest and tastiest of fare, and they bake round-cake every day. Now there's a place for a feast!"

"Enough of your talk!" snapped Willowkin who was uncommonly thin and emaciated. "As it is, you're fat enough. Mind you don't forfeit your office, and our Gracious Lord appoints someone else to hold up his robe!"

"Kings aren't so easy to find in the countryside!" said Bluebonnet, interrupting them. "But perhaps this honest wight is taking us to some prince?"

"Princes also have great palaces, courtiers, and master chefs," put in Firebrand. "They have orchestras and plenty of music; their tables groan under the weight of the silver bowls and winecups, and every night they burn enough candles to light up seven churches! They sleep long hours and make merry the livelong day. Aye, we'd be sitting pretty there. But then princes' palaces don't grow on trees. They're not like the public houses that dot the countryside. You'd have to travel far to find a prince!"

"Then perhaps he's taking us to some count!" said Willowkin. "Counts live high on the hog as well, and keep large retinues."

"*I'll* say!" put in Hempkin. "And what stables they have! What horses! What hounds!"

"Yes, but how do they eat?" asked Tubkin anxiously.

"Counts eat as counts do! How else? They have excellent kitchens where they roast wild boar and haunches of stag on spits; their pastry cooks bake tortes and create fanciful sugar cones; the servants pour golden wine out of demijohns; and the pike they bring to the table come on platters *this* big!"

And he spread his arms to their full extent, so that the Gnomes began to shake their heads with amazement.

On hearing these wonders, Peterkin, who took to everything like a spark, suddenly leapt from his seat, and tugging at Gelp's elbow called out:

"I say, good wight! Would you happen to know of a count living in these parts?"

"A count?" said Gelp, scratching himself behind the ear. "There are no counts here!" Then pausing a moment he corrected himself: "Ah yes! There's an old ruin of a building on the hill yonder—actually, nothing more than a bare chimney stack and the remains of a wall. People say counts used to live there, but now it's just a pile of rubble. The townspeople go there for bricks when they need them. The counts died out ages ago."

"Died out!" exclaimed Tubkin with lively sympathy, clapping his hands. "See how these wights depart and leave their earthly goods behind! Well, if that's so, then let our driver take us to some squire's manor! We'll come to no harm there. A country squire's a lord in his own right."

"Indeed he is!" said Bluebonnet. "In springtime he rises at dawn. He goes out into the green fields where the lark peals his blithe song; the dewfall casts pearls around his feet; flowers crochet patterned rugs over the meadows; shining shares turn up the black loam; the oxen bellow; the plowmen cry out. It's enough to make the soul swell and the heart leap with joy! In summer, our squire takes his long gun and heads for the wetland. He shoots a wild duck, straps it neatly to his bag, then gazes up at the blue sky. Nothing but happy thoughts! All around him the cornfields nod their tasseled ears; the dark-blue flax blossoms; the meadow grasses waft their fresh scent; berries redden; bees buzz in the limes . . . Then autumn! Apples, pears, and plums hang heavy on the boughs, brown boletes[1] fill the birch groves with their earthy smell, and the harvest wreath turns gold and shimmers with ears of grain, flowers, and clusters of nuts. The morning mist hangs over the fields. The sun scarcely peeps over the horizon when our squire rides out to the forest with his hunting party. The forest listens raptly to the music of the hounds. A black-eyed squirrel watches the hunters from a branch above. Suddenly, a gun

---

1    The *boletus edulis*, a species of wild mushroom.

fires—once, twice! Bang! Bang! Bang! The echoes carry far. Joyful shouts ring out, bugles blare . . ."

"Ah, bravely said, my faithful Bluebonnet!" said King Glistel, who had been listening quietly to the Gnomes' conversations. And with a wistful smile spread over his wrinkled face, he added: "May we happen upon such a manor on our journey! And even should the company there prove less than affable and genial, I shall be glad all the same!"

Just as the old King was saying this, the wagon ran over a stone and, lurching sideways, turned off the highroad onto a field path. Gelp's old nag began to snort as horses do when they smell home. At last, pulling up, the peasant turned to his passengers.

"Alight, O King," he announced, "and all the rest of you. Alight! We have arrived!"

"Where? How?" cried the Gnomes, peering out of their hoods. "But there's nothing here!"

"What do you mean nothing?" said Gelp. "This is my homestead. What did you expect?"

And, suddenly, as the night sky brightened and the air cleared itself of the shadows, the Gnomes saw before them a wretched mud hut enclosed within a leaning wattle fence overgrown with tall weeds. The hut, woven out of brushwood, was covered with a sagging, leaky roof patched up here and there with branches and wads of straw. Lording it over the weeds reared a willow-tree with its limbs outstretched like long arms. In the overgrown orchard yonder grew cherry-trees blossoming with white flowers, and over all this you could hear the chorus of countless frogs and the clacking of a nightingale, who stirring in the alders, broke out into her morning song.

"Heavens!" cried the Gnomes. "Wight! Are you making fun of us? Are you asking us the way?"

"Why should I ask the way!" said Gelp airily. "This is my homestead! Yonder's the stream. There's the grove! Who wants to, let him come. Who doesn't, then God speed him elsewhere!"

He began to unharness his nag, then going over to the well lowered the sweep, filled the bucket and calmly emptied it into the drinking trough, as though his guests were of no account.

"How shall we feed ourselves here?" asked the Gnomes.

"My children get by, and so can you!" said the peasant, filling the bucket again. "Whom God puts on this earth, he sustains in their dearth!"

"But where will we store our treasure?" they cried.

"A poppy holds a hundred times a thousand seeds and has room to spare!"

"And our King? Where shall we quarter our King?"

"The sun's a greater king, yet he scorns not my poverty. Every day he graces my homestead with his golden light . . ."

Then Peterkin, who was a merry soul and always accepted good and bad fortune with equal courage, began to dance around the wagon and sing out gaily:

> A plot of ground beneath our feet,
> A scrap of sky above our heads,
> Rejoice, my fellow Gnomes, rejoice!
> What more should we little folk want?

But this was not a time for levity, cried some, and at once a great murmur of discontented voices arose. Suddenly, the

Morning Star shone out in the eastern sky, and with it spread a splendid glow lighting up the world. At this King Glistel raised his scepter and said:

"Blest be this needy nook where toil and misery reside, for God's bright star shines over it!"

And the Gnomes fell silent.

* * *

Softly the low lindenwood door creaked open; softly, accompanied by Dawn's pearly light, they crept into Gelp's humble home. The hovel consisted of a single room. Want and misery leapt out from every corner. A massive shelved stove took up most of the space. A ginger cat lay curled up in front of it; beside it lay a bundle of dry brushwood. Farther off stood a water pail, a tin wash-bowl, and a bench with a row of pots ranged upside down on top, and next to the bench stood a deal table, two stools, and a small basket containing a few potatoes.

Struck by the misery of the house, yet loath to speak out in the King's presence, the Gnomes stood wringing their hands, nudging each other with their elbows, indicating with their eyes the huge, bare stove, the rickety bench, the wretched little basket—evidently Gelp's only pantry. Their Gnomish noses grew longer, their moustaches drooped, their brows furrowed, their lips pouted, and muffled mumblings could be heard behind their sharp, tightly clenched teeth.

But Peterkin, ever jolly and good-humored, began to run about and poke his nose into every corner.

"Now here's a palace for you!" he cried, laughing and rubbing his hands. "What lordly chambers! Why, this will do us nicely! How lively! A royal dwelling! Look! Dawn shines through the roof! See the roses she showers down? Red and golden roses! Look! See the swallow's house hanging under the rafter? It comes to life. Hear the twittering? Listen! The very rafters sing! The whole ceiling's alive with birds' feathers! Look! Look! A lilac bush bursting in through the broken window! What fragrance! What freshness! What flowers! Why, it's decked with diamonds! A rainbow on every gem! Don't tell me it's dew! No! No! Not dewdrops but precious stones! Listen! A nightingale sits in the bush. She sounds her morning song!"

Then peering into one corner, he noticed two little boys sleeping on a scattering of straw on the floor. Their fair heads lay sunk in the golden straw, and with their tattered nightshirts drawn up to their chests you could see their thin, swarthy little bodies. Evidently, the cool night air was blowing on them, for the boys held close together in each other's arms.

"Heavens!" cried Peterkin. "And what have we here? Two young princes!"

The Gnomes crowded round to look, and immediately a wistful tenderness began to smooth their brows and soften their features.

"Why, the poor little dears! How sad! Poor little waifs!" they said in whispers that grew increasingly louder.

But then King Glistel, lowering his scepter over the sleeping boys' heads, blessed them, saying:

"Grow strong in the poverty of your house! Grow strong in the shade of these lilacs and limes. Grow strong under Dawn's rosy light and the twittering of swallows! Grow so as to have the strength to shore up this sagging roof and plaster these walls! Grow strong!" And he touched the boys' fair heads with his golden scepter.

Suddenly, Gelp, who'd finished attending to his horse in the stable, appeared at the door.

"Praised be the Lord!" he said, ducking his head under the low lintel, and entering in tossed his hat on the table. At once the Gnomes made way for him and asked curiously:

"Whose are these children?"

"Whose do you think?" said the peasant. "God's first, then mine! There were more, but God took them away when their mother died. Only these two survive."

"Then may they grow up strong and healthy!" said King Glistel; and signaling to his attendants he bade them bring in the treasure and pile it by the stove.

In no time the Gnomes lugged in the chests and caskets, piled them by the stove, then dragged them into the mouse-holes—executing all this without stirring the sleeping cat.

Gelp watched them with scant interest, for now, in the full light of day, he had seen what kind of treasure he had in his wagon. Why, those little caskets were filled with dross and pebbles, nothing more! All that luster! All that radiance! All those fires and colors that had dazzled him during the night! Nothing but pebbles and dust! And those bars of silver and gold—reeds and stalks!

The unloading and storing completed, Glistel and his Gnomes disappeared into the mouseholes and began explor-ing the underground passages in and around the house. Meanwhile, Gelp turned his attention to his boys.

"Hey, Conrad! Hey, Daniel!" he yelled. "Get up, you scalawags! Don't you see your father's home?"

The boys sat up in the straw, rubbing their eyes.

"Papa! What did you bring us from the bazaar?" they said in sleepy voices.

But the peasant was in low spirits, not at all in the mood for talk.

"A birch for whacking!" he said sternly.

Then suddenly little Conrad sat up in the straw.

"Papa, I saw a king," he said.

"You saw a king? What kind of king?"

"You know, like on Twelfth Night!"

"Ah well then, it was only a dream!" said Gelp, anxious that the boys know nothing about the Gnomes and not tell the neighbors.

"But it wasn't a dream, Papa!" insisted the boy. "I really did see a king! He wore a golden crown and purple robe, his beard hung down to his waist, and he held a gold scepter that gave off a light as bright as the sun. Really, Papa, I did see a king! Wherever he went he scattered gold."

And he began to beat his breast, swearing he hadn't dreamed it.

But Gelp stamped the ground angrily with his foot.

"Enough of your dreams, lay-a-bed!" he snorted, "or you'll get such a whacking you'll dream of a stick! Now get up quickly, both of you, go fetch firewood from the forest, as we're running low! You hear me?"

"Yes, Papa," said Conrad, and at once they climbed out of the straw, washed themselves in the wooden pail, girt their caftans, and kneeling down said their prayers; then after kissing their father's hand and thrusting a few of yesterday's potatoes into their bosoms, they made for the door.

"Now, mind this, both of you,! Not a peep about any king, or—see this birch?—there'll be hell to pay! You hear me?" And he flourished his switch.

"Oh, yes, yes!" said the boys timidly. "We won't say a word to anyone. We promise, dear Papa!"

"All right, then!" said their father, tossing the birch on the bench. "Now off with you, for brushwood!"

And off went the boys. But on rounding the fence and looking cautiously back at the house, Conrad nudged his little brother, and said:

"But, you know, I really did see a king!"

* * *

Nowhere in the world could King Glistel have chosen a more delightful nook in which to establish his summer quarters. His exploration of the underground passages around poor Gelp's house, brought him out into a charming little dell. Nestled in the cool green shade of a veritable forest of burdock leaves, it stood between Gelp's overgrown cherry orchard and the dark-blue stream that wound its way across a stretch of low meadowland. Abutting it on one side was Gelp's hut; on the other side lay an abandoned strip of land where dandelions and yellow mullein grew so thick in the bent grass that the field, unworked for so long, glittered silver and gold. On the narrow balk separating the strip from a stand of alders grew hawthorn-trees awash in delicate pink flowers. How many nightingales sang there all night, and how many answered them from the alders nearby, no one could tell. A mighty chorus of frogs and the water hens and teal nesting among the reeds and rushes by the dark-blue stream tried to outshout them, but of course they couldn't. The frogs and the water fowl chorused in their way, the nightingales in theirs. And so it went all night long.

Nor did the proximity of poor Gelp's hut disturb them. Anybody unaware of its presence could walk right past and not see it, so well did the weeping willows' branches and tall grasses conceal it, so low to the ground it stood. Only at noon when Gelp boiled potatoes for himself and his children would a wreath of smoke rising through the dense vegetation betray the presence of human habitation. Even a dog wouldn't bark there, for there was nothing to feed him, nor would he have anything to guard. A person with evil intent would never peer into such a hovel, and a traveler would pass it by.

But though they murmured at this poverty, the Gnomes soon warmed to their new surroundings. These good and merry little folk love freedom above all, and only its absence makes them sad. Here, in this quiet dell overgrown with weeds and flowers, there was no one to disturb them, no one to spy on or startle them. Naming it "Nightingale Dell," they took to it even as they had to their native Grotto. Not that it was easy at first. Their first days were spent in a good deal of heavy labor and going hungry.

The first order of business was to decide on private quarters for the King who, owing to his advanced years and royal office, could hardly be expected to sleep under the burdock leaves with his entourage. The Gnomes fussed over this greatly, shaking their heads, tramping up and down the glade. For a better view Peterkin climbed a willow-tree of mighty girth and noticed that the trunk was quite hollow. Right away it occurred to him that with a little effort it could be turned it into a royal apartment; and so the Gnomes set busily to work. Some cleaned out the rotted trunk, others brought in whatever could serve for comfort and adornment. By evening of the same day King Glistel had at his disposal a magnificent apartment—beautiful, quiet and cozy. The entire interior was lined with green and russet moss; sheer lace drapery made of glassy, iridescent, spider-spun silk covered the walls; at the entrance hung an arras[2] woven out of silvery bent grass, and field flowers and herbs filled the royal residence with their marvelous scent.

The old King removed his golden crown from his weary brow, hung it on a burl, and placed his scepter in a corner. At once, the diamond ball mounted on it began to pulsate with such dazzling light you fancied the chamber were ablaze with sunlight. But since the old King's eyes were tired from gazing at the things of this world, he had the diamond covered with an alder leaf, so that the light diffused through it was muted to something more like moonlight; and in this soft, greenish light, the venerable King rested his eyes, musing fondly on the long years of his life spent performing good deeds for human folk and gathering up earth's treasures, so as to prevent them from falling into wicked hands and serving evil men.

Meanwhile, his loyal attendants, always at His Majesty's beck and call, bivouacked outside among the sturdy roots of the willow-tree. They arranged comfortable quarters for

---

2    A rich tapestry.

themselves such as gave them shelter in the rain, shade in noon sun, and a place from which to gaze at the bright stars at night—a favorite past-time of the Gnomes.

Rather more difficult was the business of finding food. For a day or two the situation was so dire that Tubkin, who couldn't endure an empty stomach, would burst into tears. But even he came up with good advice. On looking around, the Gnomes discovered that the dell, though deserted and run wild, also had its stock of resources, and not just any resources. In the alder grove grew yellow fox-cups;[3] wild strawberries and blackberries were just ripening; here and there in the old over-grown orchard a sweetish resin seeped from the bark of the cherry-trees; all manner of tasty seeds could be found in the maturing bent grass (water fennel, especially, produced them in abundance); young clover leaves made for a marvelous salad; and many roots that when scrubbed clean tasted every bit as good as choice spring asparagus. The Gnomes would then feast on this abundance. Before long, no one had to go far afield to find a special tidbit for the King.

In this Peterkin was especially tireless. Now he'd produce a bird's egg, now he'd snare a sparrow out of the great many inhabiting a nearby poplar, now with a hollowed reed he'd suck out a few drops of honey from a wasp's nest—all this just for the old King.

But with the growth of their domestic economy, it was time to think about a decent kitchen. Until then they had been cooking on a flat stone, but the dew and the rain kept put-ting the fire out. In no time Peterkin found a huge whorled

---

3   The chanterelle mushroom.

seashell, long since vacated by its owner, fashioned a stove in it out of clay and sand, closed it with little doors, and arranged a kitchen inside such as you'd be hard put to find in the whole wide world! And since, as the proverb goes, "a smoking chimney draws many friends" this is precisely what happened here too.

For many years a family of frogs had made their home under a burdock leaf by the stream. To this family belonged the bullfrog Half-Lord. Now Half-Lord was a vain and conceited fellow, full of swagger and self-importance. Sad it is, but I've nothing good to say about this Half-Lord. When I think of him, I must see him as he really was—proud and puffed up like a blowfish! No frog on his side of the stream could so swell up his throat and boast so loudly about himself as he. All day long he did nothing but sit in the sun and brag, to anyone who cared to listen, about his noble family, his marvelous voice, his intelligence and musical talent. An awful blowhard! Often he could be heard all the way from the neighboring village. This Half-Lord would foist himself upon the Gnomes, sing his own praises, and flatter his hosts while sniffing the air to see where the roast would be coming from. Sometimes he'd bring his fiddle along to entertain the Gnome King at his supper and cheer him with his music. The Gnomes held numerous functions, and this frog would be sure to be there, puffing himself up, as if he were not just half but a full, dyed-in-the-wool lord! Smoke would then billow from the kitchen that Peterkin had so artfully contrived. There was plenty to eat and drink, and the delightful smells would carry so far that the ginger cat dozing before the stove in poor Gelp's hut bristled and sniffed in his sleep, and Conrad and Daniel, hungry and clinging to each other in the straw, asked, "What's that delicious smell?"

# 6

# Maestro Sarabanda's Concert

———————

But the old King was thinking up ways to repay poor Gelp for quartering his court in his humble precincts. Gnomes are loath to give away the gold, silver, and precious gems entrusted to their care. They prefer to help the laborer in his toil, as this ennobles both the worker and the helper. But how to help poor Gelp in his work when he himself didn't know where to turn a hand? Such was the impoverished state of his homestead! Whenever Gelp came home and saw the sweepings in the corners, the dirty cobwebs in the rafters, the crumbling brick stove, the pile of ashes in front of it, the unsteady bench and table, and the grimy walls, he would drop his arms in despair.

"This poverty's beyond my strength!" he'd say to himself. "Even if I did clean up the place what good would it do? I'd still be no better off. Aah! Think I'll have a smoke instead."

And he'd light his pipe or throw himself on his bed and go to sleep.

Now Gelp was not a bad man, but he felt so crushed by want and misery that he hadn't the strength to raise himself up; he'd simply lost faith in himself. With a deal of work that little field lying in fallow could feed him and his children, but it was full of tree-stumps, rocks, muddy pools, and large shrubs, and he hadn't the strength!

"If I had one bed just for potatoes," he'd say to himself, I'd be better off than on that field! There it's root upon root, rock upon rock! Even if I worked myself to the bone I couldn't manage on my own. Before taking to the plow, I'd have to dig it all up, drain it, clear the stumps, cart off the rocks, and chop down the shrubs! And what have I got for tools? I haven't even a decent ax! Or a spade! Or plow! Or harrow! I've only the strength to dig up a few potatoes, and what? Eat them plain, without salt? No! No! I haven't the strength!"

And so he'd harness his nag to the wagon and drive to town to earn a few groats. Paltry earnings! By the time he'd had a bite to eat there, bought a handful of oats for his horse, paid the turnpike fee, and then stopped in at the tavern for a noggin, he'd have spent it all. And so went the vicious cycle. Rarely would he bring anything back in the wagon for his children.

Seeing as poor Gelp's only source of wealth were his nag and wagon, King Glistel began by ordering the Gnomes to brush down the horse beautifully every night with his own brush, comb out its mane and braid it, bring it fresh spring water and the tenderest grass, fill the stable rack with clover, lay down a bedding of moss and pine needles, chase away the flies and gnats, and even train the horse to gait properly. The villagers, who'd known the nag from before, were amazed at the change they saw in her.

"Hey, Gelp!" they called out. "Bought a new horse, eh? And forked out a pretty penny on top of the old nag!"

But Gelp only smiled. Hadn't it been passed down from his great-grandfather's grandfather that wherever Gnomes lived nearby, the horse in the stable stood sleek as a noodle, and water dripped off its coat like rain off a duck's back?

And now Gelp's wagon stood in better condition, too. Every night, the peasant's yard came alive with bright lights and happy chatter! Here Bluebonnet would be cleaning the wheels, Willowkin repairing the half-basket, Tubkin greasing the axles, and Firebrand stirring the fire and beating a new tongue on his own anvil. A regular hive of industry! And while the King's attendants worked so diligently at night, the King himself would go out alone in the early morning and keep a watchful eye over the Gelp boys collecting firewood in the forest.

* * *

Dark and silent stood the forest. Only the wind could be heard stirring above the tree-tops, speaking great and mighty words. Suddenly, what seemed like two beams of sunlight burst into that chilly gloom: it was golden-haired Conrad and little Daniel in their linen caftans girt with bright embroidered sashes. Barefoot down the path they ran, laughing and chatting in their thin childish voices. Instantly, the forest fell silent as if to eavesdrop on these little intruders. The vast canopy of the pines opened up over their golden heads; the great-girthed oaks leaned toward them; the trembling leaves of the silver birches began to whisper; and from the farthest and darkest brakes there came a soft, gentle voice, "Children! Children! Children!"

But even in these soft whispers there was something frightening. Like fledgling birds brought into a dark room, the boys fell silent in the somber gloom. But then, wonder of wonders! The lads always had to tramp all over the forest to find a stick of firewood, but now wherever they looked they found a dry branch, neither too big nor too small, but just the right size for them to carry with ease. You'd think the wind had blown them down especially for them. And what nice, resinous ones!—all beaded with sap that shone like amber. What a merry fire they'd have crackling in the stove with branches like these! Delighted, the boys laid their lengths of rope on the path and began piling on the dry branches. And how quickly and effortlessly it all went! Then another wonder! There, glistening among the dry leaves on the path, lay one of last year's hazelnuts. Had the wind blown it down? Had a squirrel dropped it while darting through the trees? The boys cracked it open on a stone and shared the sweet white kernel between them. Then they found another! Then a third! Then a whole pile of them!—all of the choicest sort! The boys were even more delighted. Little Daniel dashed off like a young hare; he shot into the undergrowth whence all you could hear was his thin little voice, shouting: "Hooray! Hooray! Hooray!" Then suddenly he gave out a scream:

"Yikes!"

Conrad ran into thicket after him. He found his little brother with his mouth quivering, unable to speak from fright.

"What did you scream for?" he asked.

"The King! I saw the King! He had a golden crown and was standing behind that red bush over there, shining bright like a fire!"

"Where?" asked Conrad.

"Why, there . . . right there!" he said, pointing with his finger. Then suddenly looking down by the bush, he cried out:

"Look, berries!"

They looked. True enough, there were bright red berries all around as if someone had scattered them there. Unheard of! There were never any berries in the forest, and now see what lay there! Forgetting their fright, the boys began gobbling them down. Never in their lives had they tasted such excellent, such sweet red berries!

After eating their fill, they tied up their faggots, and prepared to return home. Usually, this meant a good bit of straining and grunting. Not easy lifting these bundles onto their backs and then bearing them home, but now they seemed only half as heavy.

"Maybe we didn't gather enough today?" said Conrad. "My load seems so light."

"Maybe eating all these nuts and berries made us stronger?" suggested little Daniel. Then falling silent for a moment, he said:

"Conrad!"

"What!"

"Don't say anything about the King when we get home, or Papa will get mad again."

"I won't say a word!" replied his brother.

And so they set out for home.

A group of village women passing them on the way stopped and looked back.

"Aren't those the Gelp boys?" said one. "How they've changed! They look sturdier, somehow, their faces seem brighter. You'd swear it wasn't them!"

"What's to wonder about?" said another. "Maybe the Lord Jesus allows their mother to visit them at night and care for them. God knows?"

"Aye, God knows!"

And shaking their heads they went on their way.

No one knew that it was the Gnome King watching over the orphans in return for the hospitality he was receiving. But this return of a kindness seemed too little for the old King, such was the grateful heart that beat in his breast. He began to think of ways of enticing poor Gelp to work on the abandoned field and how he might help him in the labor.

One evening, when Gelp was driving home and the moon was high, he looked and saw the field all silvery in the moonlight, as when the rye stands ripe and nods its spikes in the soft breeze. So magical was the sight that he drew up sharply, jumped out of the wagon and ran into the field, scarcely believing his eyes. His heart beat loudly in his ears. For a moment he was so filled with hope that he imagined he'd sown the ground himself and was seeing its early yield. But when he looked more closely, he saw it was only the silver bent grass reflecting the bright moonlight. He sank his head, stood there for a moment, then heaving a sigh returned to his wagon.

But the vision of the field with its standing crop of silver rye wouldn't go away. That night he dreamed about it. Not long afterwards, when walking to the forest—he'd broken the shaft of his wagon and had to find a beam for a new axle—Gelp was suddenly struck by another marvelous display of light. He looked and saw the field glittering bright gold just as when the yellow wheat stands ready for the scythe, heavy with ears of white grain. The peasant stood stupefied. He looked. Shivers ran up his spine. Ye gods! It could only be wheat! But then going over for a closer look, he saw that it was only the morning sun gilding the field with its golden rays. He stood there for a moment, deep in thought, wringing his hands so hard you could hear the joints crack; and he sighed and returned home. But this new vision would appear to him not only at night but in his waking dreams. Wherever he went, wherever he sat or stood, he'd picture the wheat field and never stop thinking about it.

"Well?" he'd say to himself. "Maybe there *was* wheat cultivated there, too? Who knows? Perhaps it was? After lying fallow for so many years, the soil must be very fertile here! No one in living memory has ever sown or reaped it . . . Hmm, I wonder! . . ."

And now poor Gelp would spend hours walking around the field, assessing and re-assessing the work needed to turn it back into arable ground. "Too much, too much!" he'd mutter to himself, staring at the mighty stumps with their massive root systems, the shrubbery run wild, the huge half-sunken rocks. "Ayc! Too much, far too much!" he sighed, and he'd walk away. But scarcely would he walk away when something would lure him back again, and he'd look at the wild shrubs, then sigh, shake his head and mutter, "Too much, too much! No! I haven't the strength!"

This went on for several weeks. The peasant grew thin and emaciated from the war he was waging in his mind, he being at once drawn to this scrap of ground and repelled by it. Sometimes he resisted the temptation to go there for several days, but then it felt as if he were abandoning his possessions. Indeed, these visions were becoming increasingly vivid.

He could almost hear the wheat and the rye swishing in the field. "Pff! What is this?" he'd say. "Some kind of spell?" And he'd turn to other work.

Fortunately, there was a lumber mill just starting up at the far end of the forest by a little river close to the highroad. A great deal of timber had to be brought there in order to be cut into long, broad beams and boards. Gelp was only too glad to hire out his nag and wagon and earn a bit of money. He even managed to put some of it aside, dropping it into a pot, which he kept hidden in the rafters under the thatch. But this didn't satisfy him half as much the thought of what he could earn by selling his own grain crop. After all, who had earned this money? He and his nag! What if he or his horse should fall sick, what then? He wouldn't live forever, and a horse's span of days was even shorter than a man's. What would happen to his little boys? Destitution, that's what! But if he had some workable farmland, oh! then there'd be something for the children. And so, returning home one evening after a day's heavy work in the forest, he forced himself to go the field and gaze over it; and the old King, watching him, rubbed his hands, in high hopes that the visions induced by those magical displays of sun- and moonlight had worked their charm and roused the peasant to action.

* * *

One fine day there came to Nightingale Dell the famous traveling musician Sarabanda. No one in the district held a candle to this maestro of maestros, not even Yankel the Jew who played the bass viol in the tavern on Sundays, or Franek, who played his fiddle at every village wedding. Perhaps, perhaps! young Bartek, who spent the livelong day playing his willow pipe, equaled him in musicianship—but then not in every respect. Let no one be surprised that this maestro in his gray frock coat looked like an ordinary field cricket. He who looks deeper and probes the essence of things is not deceived by appearances. The truth of it was that Maestro Sarabanda sang beautifully. So loudly and resonantly did he chirp and play that you could hear him not just across the field but deep down in your very soul; and since any music that moves the soul expresses itself in its own words, so it was the case here.

Now when Yankel the Jew ran his bow over the strings of his bass viol, you could hear it booming a mile away:

> *Drink up, my boy!*
> *Drink up, my lad!*
> *Death comes a-rigging,*
> *Your grave he's digging,*
> *Death comes a-rigging,*
> *Your stone he's sprigging,*
> *Yours but the lees*
> *Left in the jug! . . .*

And when Franek and his drummer led the wedding party through the village, you could hear his fiddle laugh out and sing:

> *A golden ducat*
> *For a dance!*
> *A silver florin*
> *For a fiddle!*

*Who thought up Toil?*
*Some old curmudgeon*
*No girl would think*
*Of dancing with!*

And young and old would drop their work and dash off to the wedding hall and sneak peeks at the wallflowers. All work in the village would cease for a day or two or three, and time would blithely come and go, taking with it what little remained of the village's meager stores.

Or again, when the shepherd-boy Bartek played his pipe, the hearts of the people would grow immeasurably sad, as if someone were grieving and sobbing. Then you could hear the pipe moan:

*Misery stalks my house,*
*Our ground yields meager grain,*
*The wind sweeps o'er the fields,*
*Sows tares among the corn.*

*O bitter, bitter lot!*
*I will not reap these fields;*
*To warmer lands I'll sail*
*And bask there in the sun! . . .*

Hearing these strains of Bartek's pipe, the field folk would drop their tools, for the plow would seem unbearably heavy, the soil hard and unyielding, the scythe-blade blunt, the straw stiff and unbending; and all the strength would flow out of their hands as if dreary toil had drained it to the dregs.

Not so with Maestro Sarabanda! He stood so close to the ground that he knew the soil's strength, its goodness—its sweetness! Every morning and evening when he sang of the fields, meadows, forests and streams, he'd tug at your very heart-strings.

One day while sitting and musing wistfully on his doorstep, Gelp felt his heart overflow with a warm love for the humble inheritance his fathers had left him. The sun was setting, and the Gnomes had come out to watch the flaming ball, to enjoy its afterglow and the cool, pristine air. Maestro Sarabanda came out, too, to watch the evening spectacle. Mounting a hummock in the glade, he began to play his magical fiddle and sing.

Gelp listened with rapt attention. What he heard were like silver gusli strings ringing in the air, sounds resolving themselves into tender words and flowing from deep within the heart—the very soul. He listened on. The sounds grew louder, ranging ever wider until they burst like organ music over the fields and forests, embracing the rivers, meadows and streams, stirring the leaves of the field pears and forest oaks, whispering in the meadow grasses . . . In the quiet of that evening the mighty music seemed to draw from the breast a choir of a million voices, as though not one, but a million hearts were beating within it:

> *Earth! Sweet, neglected earth!*
> *Silver and gold you yield,*
> *Grain plentiful for all,*
> *But first you must be loved!*

*O earth! Sweet mother earth!*
*You feed and nourish all,*
*Give life its force and strength,*
*Raise flowers from the grave!*

*Sweet earth! Beloved earth!*
*No plowshare breaks your ground,*
*No harrow smooths your loam,*
*No gold in you is sown!*

A surge of strength flowed into the peasant's soul as never before. Never before had he felt such a strong sense of attachment to that scrap of ground. Suddenly, it seemed he had a hundred arms, a hundred hands, ripe and ready for the great undertaking of grubbing, plowing, harrowing, and sowing; and his heart melted with a burning love for his birthright and humble inheritance. Rising to his feet, he gazed at the world with a strong, determined eye, stretched forth his arms, clenched his fists, and muttered:

"Sweet earth, sweet earth! Work! Work! You frighten me no more. Either you'll conquer me, or I you! . . . So help me God!"

# 7

# Bluebonnet and His Student

_____

But Half-Lord was not at all impressed with Maestro Sarabanda's performance. Green as Mother Nature had made him, he became twice as green with envy.

"Egads!" he cried. "That some itinerant cricket should seek accolades in a country where all applause rightfully belong to me! Who gave him the right to wander in here, stupefy his listeners with his shrill creakings and ruin their taste for my music? Why, it's outrageous!"

And turning to Bluebonnet who'd heard his remonstrations he said:

"Sir, if you'd be so kind as to fetch me this interloper's score, you'll see how I outperform and put him to shame! When I've taught myself that piece, the whole world will know who the _real_ maestro is. Be so kind, dear sir! Help me in this, I beg you!"

Being an obliging soul, Bluebonnet ran up at once to the departing musician. Seizing him by the tails of his frock coat, he begged him for the score of the beautiful song whose echoes could still be heard reverberating in the field herbs and dew-covered grasses.

"There lives among us a very talented frog," he explained. "We have a mind to appoint him court musician for our gracious lord and King. Being advanced in years, His Majesty is given to spells of longing and sadness. Such an excellent musician would comfort him in his periods of melancholy."

"Why, by all means!" said Sarabanda. "Here's the score, take it, please take it! . . . Mind you, it doesn't contain the whole song. The rest of it, the part that's missing, has to come from the soul. Oh, but that presents no difficulty! All you need do is gaze at the glow of the sunset, smell the scent of meadow grass, and listen to the ringing silence of the fields . . . Easy, very easy! Here's the score, take it, please take it! The pleasure's mine. Your humble servant!"

And placing the score in Bluebonnet's hand, the great musician departed, leaving the Gnome standing in wonderment that this maestro of maestros should be so kind and obliging, and, at the same time, so modest, so plain-spoken—awkward, even!

"Well!" he said to himself. "Half-Lord is right! If a humble cricket is capable of producing such sublime music, then what of our frog, who so exceeds him in size, personality and sheer presence?"

And with the score clutched in his hand he ran back to Nightingale Dell where Half-Lord stood waiting for him.

May was just ending and it was hot in the world when our green blowhard began rehearsing his concert. Choosing a spot under a mushroom at the very edge of the stream, he seated himself there, as though under a parasol, and practiced the Maestro's piece every day. But alas! He was always losing the rhythm. Bluebonnet, wilting under the fierce sun and dripping with sweat, was forced to beat out the tempo for him, using a broken reed for a baton. Horrendous rehearsals these! No describing the screeching, the raspings, the jarring false notes! The frog went on torturing the piece while Bluebonnet flailed with his baton like three washerwomen at the riverside beating their wash with laundry paddles; meanwhile, with a whine and a buzz and a flutter of wings, beetles, flies, gnats, and even the sparrows fled in every direction—anywhere just to put distance between their ears and the hapless mushroom under which the frog was seated. But not everything could get away.

Bluebonnet was forced to beat out the tempo for him, using a broken reed for a baton.

By the bank of the same stream there were water lilies not permitted to leave their cool, blue dwelling-place. Unable to escape the awful noise, they drooped their white petals and begged desperately for a moment of peace and quiet.

"Pardon us, dear benefactors!" they said in a sweet, polite voice. "But ever since you gentlemen have been devoting your-selves to your music, our convent has been in a state of constant commotion as though we were living in a watermill. We mean no disrespect to you sirs, but we find ourselves unable to pray to the morning sun, or hear the maybells ring for vespers in the grove yonder. Our daily regimen's been turned upside-down . . . You gentlemen must surely know that we weave silver threads on looms for our novices sequestered in their green cells, but even the threads on our looms are bursting from the unbear-able noise you are pleased to make right in front of our gate! We have tried to retreat deeper into the water where it is quieter, but we cannot live without the sun. Please do not be offended by our request! We recognize your great talent, kind sir in the green suit, as we recognize also the exertions—the very great exertions!—of you, sir, in the blue cap. But as it is, we cannot bear it! We're close to nervous collapse."

Here the lilies bowed their heads like dampened wicks and retreated meekly into the large round leaves that served them for veils.

But the reeds and the rushes were nowhere near as polite. They began at once to beat their staves and rattle their long swords.

"Who's that shrieking there?" they cried, "You'd think some-one was being flayed alive! Silence, you screecher! Here we stand, a whole army of us, a hundred voices strong, and never could we raise such an infernal racket! Hey boys, ply your staves! Let him feel the flat of our swords! Hey boys! Make music, our golden reeds! Let this shrieker know what real music is like! Drummers beat! Buglers blow! . . ."

And the bulrushes began to bend and moan, the reeds swished and rustled, the sweet flag clanked its sword-shaped leaves, and the wind made a strange music as though a thousand silver shawms[1] were piping.

> *Hey, softly! Stealthily!*
> *No noise now! Not a peep!*
> *We wait in ambush here;*
> *The password! Soft now! Speak!*

> *We wait in ambush here,*
> *Our swords are drawn and poised,*
> *The password! Soft now! Speak!*
> *You know it not? Begone!*

Strange music such as our Gypsies make, ever so quiet at first, then building up to a wild crescendo. For a while the music thundered in the bulrushes, then, growing soft again, it faded away like a passing sigh.

But Half-Lord, consumed with jealousy and pride, paid no attention either to the threats of the blusterous rushes and reeds or to the humble pleas of the water lilies. Indeed, the louder their threats and entreaties grew, the more vehemently he shrieked to drown them out, his throat swelling up like a giant balloon.

---

1   A conical bored, double-reed woodwind instrument common in the Middle Ages.

"For Heaven's sake!" cried the terrified Bluebonnet. "Restrain your singing, or you'll burst before my eyes!"

Hardly had he spoken, when . . . Bang! The membrane stretched tight as a drum-skin over his throat burst, and Half-Lord, giving out a single gasp, collapsed where he sat.

\* \* \*

The late afternoon was hot and close. A string of mowers were still plying their scythes. Their white linen smocks shone bright in the sun. Evenly they moved through the meadow: in tandem they bent forward, arms extended; in tandem they swung their glistening blades close to the ground. Under a pear-tree on the balk nearby stood several jugs containing golden potatoes and cool fermented milk. The children had brought them there from the cottages. Clad in red vests and blue skirts they were now seated together like a clump of poppies and larkspurs, playing "guess who."

Suddenly, a tiny little figure carrying a golden bowl and large golden spoon waddled out of the grove and made straight for the jugs. It was Tubkin, King Glistel's portly page. Unable to stand the heat, he'd come from the dell to refresh himself with the cool milk. The children stiffened in awe. They saw him reach for the nearest jug, dip in his spoon and ladle out the clotted milk into his bowl. He'd almost filled it and was scraping the rest of the cream from the sides of the jug when the air was suddenly rent by the cries of a hundred thin little voices:

"Our musician is dead!"

Hearing the cry, Tubkin threw down his spoon and bowl and trundled off as fast as he could back to the dell.

"A Gnome! A Gnome!" cried the children, catching sight of the red hood flapping behind him, and starting up like a flock of startled sparrows they raced back to the village, yelling at the top of their voices; and the golden bowl Tubkin had dropped rolled down the grassy slope into a sloeberry bush, and there it remained.

Great was the fuss and consternation in Nightingale Dell when Tubkin arrived. The Gnomes were trying frantically to revive Half-Lord. Some were shaking him, some rubbing him down; others turned him from side to side, still others held a smoldering crow's feather under his nose. Peterkin ran up with a cup of water, but in his haste he ended up soaking both the afflicted and his revivers. All in vain! Half-Lord lay cold and lifeless. His eyes were milky white, his legs hung limp. A corpse if ever there was one! Nothing for it but to lay him in the ground.

Now a wizened old crone happened to be gathering wild herbs in the grove nearby. Dry as a piece of brushwood and brown as a birch bolete, she was so bent over with age that she was unable to look up at the sun. She walked with a cane, tapping the ground before her, and whenever she came upon an herb, she addressed it in a soft dry voice.

"O sundew!"[2] she exclaimed upon seeing one now. "O leafy sundew! On each leaf a dewdrop sits. In each drop gleams the

---

2   The *drosera rotundifolia*, a carnivorous species of flowering plant that grows in bogs, marshes, and fens.

sun. He gives you strength, great strength! Good for ailing eyes! For young and old. Come, come you into my basket!"

And picking a handful, she walked on, muttering softly.

"O stonecrop!"[3] she said a little farther on. "My handsome young rambler! From hill to dale, from dale to hill you roam. Across dark sands you trek, heedless of where you go, for you have golden feet. Good for toothaches! Come, come into my basket!"

And she picked a few sprigs of the herb. She walked on, then stopped again.

"O thyme!" she said, twirling her cane. "My fragrant little herb! Good for every ailment, for spells of sadness and sorrow, and aching bones! Come, come you into my basket!"

She picked the fragrant leaves in silence, then leaning sideways and straightening her back a little, she surveyed the grove with her deep blue eyes and crooned:

> *A mother heard her orphans weep;*
> *From night's dark mound she reared her head*
> *E'en as the rue that peeps above.*
> *Stepmother, saw she, riding gaily,*
> *Riding gayly to wedded be,*
> *And bitterly the orphans wept,*
> *And bitterly the orphans wept.*

Her feeble voice echoed through the grove then faded away; and heaving a sigh, she stooped her shoulders and plodded on. But then again she stopped and twirled her cane.

---

3 The *sedum spurium* or *orpine*, a mat-forming, creeping, upright plant.

*O touchwort[4] sweet! O darling herb!*
*As turns the Sun, so shines your face,*
*A golden brew you make: for croup*
*And coughs! Into my basket, come!*

And driving away the bees that swarmed over the long-stemmed flower, she picked a sprig or two of the herb then went on, muttering softly. Yet again she stopped.

*O wormwood! Bitterest of herbs!*
*A little sprig of you I'll pick—*
*We wights escape not bitterness!*
*Let him that ails but two drops take.*
*Come you into my basket, come!*

The touchwort and wormwood brought her out of the grove and into a glade at the very edge of the meadow where the mowers were busy reaping. Beside a field pear on the balk nearby she saw a clump of hawthorns. Going up to them, she crooned softly:

*O sturdy hawthorn! Hawthorn strong!*
*We strew your sprays before our doors*
*To keep unwelcome cares away.*
*Come you into my basket, come!*

She rested a while and looked around; then just as she was about to walk away, she saw a root sticking out of the ground. Her face suddenly brightened. Tears bedewed his eyes, and

---

4   The common mullein.

bending down she began to dig up the root, murmuring softly the while:

> *O banewort[5] fair of face!*
> *Black pots they boil you in,*
> *In dead of night they boil you*
> *To knit dead bones together.*
> *Into my basket, come!*

She began to tug at the root, but it wouldn't come out. She heard a faint cry. "What's this?" she exclaimed. "Can the root be pulling back?" And releasing it, she listened. Yes, a cry! But it wasn't the root. Those were human voices! At once she bent her steps toward the sounds, limping along as best she could, supporting herself on her cane. The voices grew louder. At last she came out, puffing and wheezing, into a dell close to a blue steam. She looked and saw a throng of Gnomes standing around a lifeless frog.

"Our musician! Our musician is dead!" they cried, sobbing and wringing their hands.

The old woman showed neither surprise, nor fear. All her life she'd lived cheek by jowl with wonders. What were wonders to her? Gnomes, too, she'd seen many times in her long life. What were Gnomes to her? . . . And so, blinking her blue eyes, she drew closer.

"Now what has the Good Lord brought here?" she asked the Gnomes

---

5   The deadly nightshade.

"Alas!" they cried. "Our musician's throat has burst! Oh please, old Mother, save our musician!"

The crone nodded her head and approached the frog. She raised its leg, then the other. Limp as old rhubarb sticks! She put her ear to its breast and listened. Then listening again, she suddenly smiled . . .

"Someone fly at once beyond the three mountains steep, beyond the three seas deep, to the wilds at the ends of the earth where stands my house! Quickly now! Fetch me my gold-eyed needle and silken thread! We may still be able to save your frog!"

At once Peterkin dashed off to Gelp's hut where he cried out to the swallow:

> O Swallow! Swallow dear!
> Take me upon your back,
> On swift wings bear me hence
> Beyond the mountains steep,
> Beyond the three seas deep.
>
> To earth's wild edges take me
> Where stands the old crone's hut.
> I must this instant fetch
> Silk thread and golden needle
> To save our stricken frog!

The swallow twittered sweetly, happy to oblige. Peterkin leapt on its back—and away they flew on the wind.

Meanwhile, the woman lit a fire, lay down some branches crosswise, boiled her herbs, and bathed Half-Lord's throat with the brew. The Gnomes helped her as best as they could. One fetched the firewood, another worked the bellows, fanning the flames, another held the pot. The Gnome King himself held up Half-Lord's head, and every time he looked at him, bright tears guttered down his whiskered face.

In less time it takes to mutter three prayers, the swallow's fleet wings were heard fluttering over the dell. Peterkin leapt lightly off its back, thanked him, and handed the old woman the gold-eyed needle and silken thread. Taking out her spectacles, she placed them on the bridge of her nose, and threading the needle proceeded to sew up the hapless frog's throat. The Gnomes crowded around her, poking their noses over the others' heads, watching intently. After sewing up Half-Lord's ruptured skin, the woman waved a valerian root under his nose and breathed on him three times. Then if the frog didn't fire off a sneeze! It was like a canon shot! The Gnomes sprang back from fright. Half-Lord opened one eye, batted his eyelid several times, then opened the other eye. He sat up, looked around him, and suddenly catching sight of the Maestro's score seized it in his webbed hand and opened his mouth to sing. He opened it, but not a sound came out! He opened it wider. Still nothing! He opened it a third time, and only a hollow squeak came out. O hapless Half-Lord! You haven't a prayer of toppling Maestro Sarabanda!

8

# At the Palace of the
# Mountain Queen

_____

For three days and three nights Little Orphan Mary journeyed to the Southern Mountains. The first day took her across open country, across fields and meadows abounding in corn, lush grass, and fragrant flowers. The whole day you could hear the grain rustling, the grasses swishing, the flowers whispering, "Orphan . . . orphan . . . orphan . . ." The grain stalks parted before her, as though the wind's mighty wings were dividing them. Moving her arms from front to back, Mary plowed through this silver forest, her skirt blue as a cornflower in the grain. On she trekked, murmuring to herself, "Lead on, lead on, dear field! Lead me to the Queen of the Southern Mountains!"

The fields guided the little wayfarer's steps. Before her ran the furrows, spilling pearls of dew; before her ran the long unplowed ridges awash in scented flowers. On she walked along soft paths flecked with forget-me-nots, and above her head a meadowlark beat its gray wings, singing, "This way, this way, sweet waif!" The field pears leaned out toward her, inviting her into their shade. Boundary mounds made her stop for brief rests by flowering bramble bushes. A black cross standing at a crossroads among three birch-trees reached out its arms, and every living creature sang and danced in the fields—birds, midges, bees, and crickets, all sounding the same note, "Onward, onward! . . ."

Everywhere quiet villages dotted the countryside. Across the length and breadth of the land lowed herds of cattle; horses whinnied in the pastures, snow-white lambs sported on the hills, shepherds' pipes echoed, and all around—nothing but blue . . . blue . . . blue . . .

Behind Mary walked Spratkin, his hood bobbing over the green meadows and fields like a red poppy, his beard upraised, for he imagined it was he that was leading her . . . But it wasn't he!

> *The field paths guided her;*
> *The bluebells' nodding heads,*
> *The insect-haunted balks,*
> *The soaring larks, the gnats*
> *All led the orphan onward;*
> *The meadow herbs bedewed*
> *With pearls, the golden dawn*
> *All guided her along.*

But on the second day Mary entered a cool, forbidding world, a world of green twilights and solemn silence—a world of forests! Great-girthed oaks bent over with age surrounded her, spreading their limbs, rustling their leafage of splendid green. Dark, stirless pines, trunks dripping with amber-gold resin, compassed her round. Among the pines stood silver birches of tender leaf, the pensive hornbeam upon whose ironwood the scythe-blade is mounted, and the low, ever-thirsty guelder-rose that stands in low-lying hollows.

On walked Mary as through a vast cathedral supported by a thousand columns, its floor flagged with patches of dark-green moss; and high above, the sun burst through the leaves, scattering nuggets of golden light. On she walked, awed by the solemn silence, all the while whispering in her heart, "Lead on, lead on, dear trees! Lead me to the Queen of the Southern Mountains!" The broad-limbed oaks, the dark pines, the white birches, the hornbeams, and the low guelder roses all answered back, raising mighty sounds in their lofty crowns, mere whispers in their lowest leafy branches. And in these sounds and whispers you could clearly make out the words, "This way! . . . this way! Go this way, little waif!"

The forest opened its vast canopy over Mary's head. The sunlight fell on the mossy path before her, as though some-one in the forest's gloom were strewing golden stars to guide her along. On she walked, intent upon her simple wistful song which the birches and the ancient oaks accompanied, whis-pering, murmuring . . .

> *O forest dark! O woodland deep!*
> *How sweet your leafy murmuring!*
> *How sweet the sounds your branches make!*
> *Oh, soft yet loud your stillness rings!*

And as she went singing, the sound of the woodsman's axe answered her from afar, a cuckoo called, a squirrel squeaked, a woodpecker tapped on a spruce stump. When, absorbed in her song, she took a wrong turn, a bramble bush snagged her skirt and stopped her, an eagle-owl, hidden in a tree-cleft, hooted, a green lizard ran across her path, and a hazelnut-tree bowed its spray over her golden head, whispering, "This way . . . this way . . . this way!"

Behind Mary walked Spratkin, his hood flashing like a red toadstool, his beard upraised, for he imagined it was he that was leading her . . . But it wasn't he.

> *The silver birches led her,*
> *The ferns, the mosses green,*
> *The thirsty guelders led her;*
> *The forest paths, the brakes,*
> *The mighty oaks, the pines—*
> *All led her on her way;*
> *Soft sighs and soughings deep*
> *Led little Mary through*
> *The forest's towering gates.*

But on the third day, Mary entered a world of mountains and streams, a world all blue with mists and distant peaks, all silvery with waters that ran wilder than in the two previous worlds. Rocky steeps as far as the eye could see! Lofty crags, one piled upon another, jutting into the sky, butting their brows against the clouds. Thundering torrents wherever you looked! Streams spurted from massive rock-faces and ran foaming and singing into the gorges. And all the while, the gold of the sun and the blue of the sky looked down; and the wind-swept clouds looked down, now obscuring the blue, now extinguishing the gold. A wild, forbidding world! Have a care, little traveler! Beware of the treacherous stream rushing over the rocks, the rumble of boulders cascading into yawning chasms, the screams of eagles balancing on heavy wings! Rocks and water everywhere! Such was this world.

On trudged Little Orphan Mary, her face drained of hue, her eyes glazed over, her heart trembling in her breast. On hand and foot she scrambled, all the while muttering, "Lead on, you mountains, guide me to the Queen of the Southern Mountains!" Now and then, the crags would part their heads to reveal below quiet sunlit dales traversed by pathways soft and grassy. Mountain freshets in full spate tumbled down, spinning threads of silver and blue. A soaring eagle screeched, and all these sounds seemed to be saying, "Onward! Onward, little waif!"

On labored Mary, dazed by the roaring waterfalls, the booming rocks, the brawling streams, the rustling of eagles' wings. On she climbed, dazed by the sheer mountains' bulk and lofty peaks that scraped the sky; dazed by their lights and shades; dazed by their might and strength—might and strength so great that the girl's little song fell silent, even as a bird's when darkness falls. With a trembling heart she soldiered on, whispering softly, "O Earth! O Earth! O Earth!"

Behind Mary walked Spratkin, his red hood waving among the rocks, his beard upraised, for he imagined it was he that was leading her . . . But it wasn't he!

> *Those lofty mountains led her,*
> *That world of towering crags!*
> *Those tumbling torrents led her*
> *Toward the royal chambers . . .*
> *The soaring eagle led her,*

*The snowcapped mountain peak,*
*The howling winds—all led her*
*Toward the golden throne*
*Where sat the Gracious Queen.*

\* \* \*

The Queen's palace stood atop a lofty peak, a mountain so high that the silver clouds lay at its feet like a flock of sheep on the green; its summit shone like the sun in the limpid sky. Two spruce forests led up toward the castle gates. Two crags—two stone titans—stood guard over the gates. Two mountain pines spread a mossy carpet over the staircase leading to the royal chambers. Two streams poured day and night out of wondrously wrought emerald-green pitchers in the antechamber. Two whirlwinds howled in the vestibule like a pair of mastiffs. Two eagles balanced above the castle turrets, and two blue stars burned in the loopholes: the Morning and the Evening Star!

Terror and rapture seized little Mary as she gazed up at the mountain before her.

"Sweet Jesus! Where have I come?" she muttered, shaken to her very soul.

And, suddenly, the air was rent by a roar as loud as a hundred thunderclaps, and the choir and the black harps of the first spruce forest burst into a booming song:

"Great and mighty is the Queen of the Southern Hills! Her head rears high above the earth! A diadem of ice rests on her head, veils of snow enfold her neck, silver mists, her shoulders! Her grim and baleful eyes flash lightnings. Her voice is the torrents' roar, the thunder's clap! Her wrath kindles firebolts, shatters trees! Her bed are the black clouds, yet sleep she vouchsafes no one. Her foot tramples every flower, every blade of grass . . . Implacable is her heart of stone! Aye, great and mighty is the Queen of the Southern Hills!"

Little Mary shuddered at the sound of the song. When it ceased, its echoes went cascading into the chasms. Down, down, like an avalanche, they rolled, threatening the silent valley below. Scarcely did the echoes die down when the choir of the second spruce forest broke forth to the accompaniment of silver lutes:

"Good and merciful is the Queen of the Southern Hills! She spins fine threads of mist, she clothes the naked crags, weaves them crowns from sprays of mountain pine and sets them on their brows. Lifeless snow she turns into sparkling springs which feed the fields and lowlands, that they may yield their harvest of grain. She provides the grizzled eagle with a home; his unfledged babes she cradles in lofty nests. The nimble mountain goat she hides in crannies hidden from the hunter's prowling eye. With tender eyes she peers into the valleys, revives the panting flower with the coolness of her breath . . . Wondrous tapestries she weaves from velvet mosses and hangs them in shadow-filled chasms. She feeds the poor that have no field or grain, instructs their tots to reach for heights . . . Aye, good and merciful is the Queen of the Southern Hills!"

The choir fell silent; the echoes sank lower and lower into the valley, becoming soft as the murmur of waters, soft as the whisper of woodland trees. All this Mary heard, and her spirits rose, and her eyes filled with grateful tears, for surely, she thought, if this queen was so good, she would not turn away a poor orphan like herself . . . She was bracing herself for the final ascent when she heard one of the two eagles address her in a human voice:

"Bravely does it, little waif."

"But the path's so steep and stony?"

"Fear not!" said the eagle. "I'll drop you one of my flight feathers. It will make the going easier."

The eagle's feather floated down and fell at Mary's feet. The orphan picked it up, pressed it to her bosom, and suddenly her step became brisk and light. She no longer felt the stones; her feet scarcely grazed the ground. You'd swear she was breasting the air. She conquered the ascent, and before she knew it found herself standing before the palace gates.

"How will I enter with all this snow and ice around?" she wondered.

And, suddenly, as she looked up, a sunbeam spoke to her in a human voice.

"Fear not! I shall warm the snow and ice."

At once a golden path appeared before her, such was the warmth the sunbeam shed. The child walked on, not feeling the cold, indeed, it was as though she were treading a carpet of white blossoms such as apple-trees shed in May. And so she arrived at the castle's antechamber. But to get beyond it she had to cross a rushing stream.

"How can I ford it?" she wondered. "I'd have to get my feet wet!"

Suddenly, as she looked up, a cloud of mist came floating down and spoke to her in a human voice:

"Fear not! Walk straight ahead! I'll throw a silver bridge over the stream."

At once the mist thickened and settled over the stream, allowing Mary to walk over it as over a silver footbridge. At last, she found herself at the threshold of the royal chambers. But here her heart was so seized by a sense of dread that she had half a mind to turn back. Fortunately, the lagging Spratkin, seeing her hesitate, dashed breathlessly up to the door, thrust it open and pulled her into the chamber. Mary gave out a cry, dazzled by the Maytime splendor and richness of the throne room where the monarch sat. She dropped her eyes, not daring to gaze into the Queen's resplendent face. All too conscious of her poverty and orphaned state, she stood motionless, unable to speak. But the Queen beckoned to her with her white hand, and said:

"Who are you, my child?"

Mary opened her mouth to reply, but her voice died in her breast. Again Spratkin stepped up. Hiding his pipe behind his back, then bowing courteously, he addressed the Queen on Mary's behalf.

"This is the little gooseherd Mary from Famine Hamlet—a poor orphan!"

He shuffled his feet and bowed again with an extravagant flourish of his arm.

The sight of the little Gnome brought a kindly smile to the Queen's lips. Turning her wondrous face to Mary, she asked:

"What is it you want, my child?"

And here, unable to hold herself back, Mary stretched out her emaciated arms and cried:

Hiding his pipe behind his back, Spratkin addressed the
Queen on Mary's behalf.

"I want my little geese, kind Queen! I want to see my seven
little geese alive again—the ones the wicked fox killed! I want
to hear my gander honk again, my geese to answer him . . . I
want to see them grazing on our little meadow . . ."

And covering her eyes with her hands, she burst into sobs,
and an ample stream of tears poured through her fingers.

Silence fell over the room as the poor orphan wept on.

Then the Queen nodded benignly and addressed her audience slowly with the following words:

"Many have come here asking for favors. They ask for gold,
for silver, for a betterment of their lot. But such as would depart

from here with what was theirs in the first place, as would this child—such I have never seen. Let it be then as you wish!"

And rising from her throne, the Mountain Queen led Mary to the window. The orphan looked out and clapped her hands in surprise . . . Was it a dream or no? From the Queen's palace she could see her village as though it were on the palm of her hand. She saw the gooseherds cracking their whips lustily, driving their flocks before them on the sandy road; and—wonder of wonders!—in the meadow by the forest she saw her seven geese grazing on the grass. The gander was honking loudly; the brindled goose was answering back. And there beside them sat her faithful little dog Oscar, staring into the forest, whimpering softly, waiting for his mistress.

"Jesu! . . . Jesu! . . ." cried Mary, at a loss for words, her heart wild with joy. "My geese alive! My little geese alive!"

* * *

Even as Little Orphan Mary cried out, shedding tears of joy, the Queen touched her and called her by name. The girl awoke and looked about her. Where was she? She was lying on a bench, on a pile of fresh hay covered with a sheet of cloth. Beside her stood a deal table with a few pots placed upside down on it. A huge shelved stove stood nearby; before it lay a ginger cat curled up in a ball; beside it lay a bundle of dry brushwood tied up with a piece of rope; farther off stood a water jug and a tin wash-bowl. The dark-leaved branches of a lilac bush poked through a broken window. Two fair-haired boys in tattered shirts open at the neck sat on wooden stools at her feet. The setting sun's roseate rays shone through the leafage, painting golden circles on the boys' sunburned chests.

Mary felt very hot; there was something tight around her head. She touched it with her hand; it was bound with a rag. On seeing her wake, both boys leapt up and knelt beside her.

"How do you feel?" said one.

"Do you want a drink?" said the other.

Mary looked at them, but they were strangers to her.

"Who are you?" she asked.

"We're Peter Gelp's young lads. He's Daniel, and I'm Conrad" said the older boy.

"But whose house is this?"

"Whose? Why, ours, of course!"

"How did I get here?"

"Papa brought you, that's how!"

"But where did he find me?"

"In the forest! He was coming back from town and was going into the forest to cut himself a new switch, as his old one was broken, and then this little yellow dog came up, whining. He started tugging on Papa's coat and made him follow him into the bushes."

"Why, that'll be my little Oscar!" cried Mary. "How is he? Has he come to any harm?"

"Oh, he's all right," said Conrad, laughing. "But then Papa found you lying there almost lifeless, so he brought you here to the house, and that's that."

"But what about my mistress?"

"Oh, forget about your mistress! You're better off here. We asked Papa not to give you back to her."

"Papa said we didn't have enough bread," added little Daniel, "but we'll share it with you anyway, as there's food now in the forest, so we won't go hungry."

"I'll say!" said Conrad. "Plenty of red and black berries, not to mention wild mushrooms, and there's last year's nuts to be found lying about."

"Papa even took the switch to us," said little Daniel, laughing. "That's how much we pleaded with him."

"Took the switch?! Whatever for?" said Mary, shocked.

"Oh, not really, but he threatened to," said Conrad laughing. "But that didn't stop us."

"So your papa decided I should stay here?"

"Well, not at first," said Conrad. "He said he'd have to go to the village and find out who you were."

"And did he?"

"Oh, yes! And he found out about your mistress, too."

"And? . . . What then?"

"Well, first she lamented that the wolves had devoured you, and then she lamented that they hadn't, and you were lying sick in our house. 'What good to me is a sick gooseherd!' she said. 'I've taken on another girl to tend the geese, and now I have to keep her.'"

"So my geese are alive?!" cried Mary joyfully, sitting up on the bench.

"Oh yes! Four white and three brindled ones."

"That's right!" said little Daniel earnestly. "And what fine birds they are!"

Mary blinked her eyes and sighed, as though a great stone were lifted from her heart. The boys told her many others things besides, but Mary no longer heard them, for sleep had suddenly seized her in her exhaustion.

When she woke up again, it was already dark. The sun had gone down, the hut was deserted. Through the half-opened door she could see the golden stars rolling across the sapphire sky, peeping in on her on their way, as if inquiring after her health. Suddenly, the door creaked open wider, and something ran into the room, knocked over the stools, and leapt up on the girl.

"Oscar! My Oscar!" cried Mary in a feeble voice, hugging her darling little dog. "So you haven't forgotten Little Orphan Mary!" A stream of happy tears fell from her eyes, as Oscar, whimpering joyously and wagging his tail, licked her sunburned little hands.

Yes, Little Orphan Mary! The world is full of wonders. Many a tear is dried by a merciful hand in golden dreams such as the one here just granted you!

\* \* \*

Meanwhile, great was the amazement in Famine Hamlet when the new gooseherd appeared driving her flock to pasture. The people stared, shook their heads, surmising one thing, then another, but never coming to any agreement.

"Are those the same geese, or not? What say you, neighbor?"

"How should I know when they keep changing before my eyes. Maybe they're the same, maybe not! The brindled one looks bigger . . . Taller somehow!"

"What do you mean bigger! To my eyes she's the smallest of the lot."

The people said all kinds of things about these geese, for they thought they were dead, yet here they were strutting about again.

"Well! Well! . . . Wonders never cease! . . ."

And the villagers walked on, shaking their heads.

But even more amazed was the fox, Greasy Tod! Creeping up, first from the left side then from the right, he stared out from the edge of forest at the new gooseherd's little flock.

"What's this?" he muttered to himself. "How can this be? Haven't I done them in once already?" (The very memory of it made him lick his cruel chops.) "How on earth did they come alive again?"

Uneasy, fearing the worst, he raced off dodging the trees toward the glade where he'd piled the bodies of the throttled birds. Looking about, he saw goose down scattered like snow over the grass, but of the birds themselves, not a trace!

"I've been robbed! . . . looted! . . . plundered!" he cried out aloud. You'd think the miscreant had been robbed of the fruits of an honest labor. And in a transport of rage he threw himself down and began rolling and tossing about in the grass.

Suddenly, he saw a small fawn animal with large roundish ears, standing upright in the tall grass before him and staring at him with a pair of sharp black eyes. Enraged at being caught in this state of desperation, the fox sprang up, and, since he was vain as he was cruel, he gnashed his teeth and screamed:

"What are you gaping at? Is this a spectacle you're watching? . . . Look at him! . . . Standing on his hind legs as though he were in a theater! You must have seen the thief stealing my geese to be staring like this, eh? Just wait! I'll skin you alive. You'll answer for this! An evil hour you've caught me in!"

He might have leapt at its throat there and then, but on hearing the fox's very first words, the hamster dropped back on his forepaws and made for its burrow, terrified at having incurred the wrath of such a beast. The fox forbore to give chase, as he'd just killed a pigeon and wasn't hungry, having crunched up the bird to the last little bone. Instead, he was content to direct a last parting threat in the direction of the grass left swaying in the hamster's tracks.

"Just wait! . . . We'll meet up again, when my belly's empty! . . . I'll reckon with you yet, you confounded little snooper! . . ."

And seething with rage, he turned back into the forest, snorting wildly.

# 9

# Midsummer's Night Eve

———————

The villagers no longer recognized their poor neighbor Gelp. After that spring night when the strains of great Maestro Sarabanda's song had so magically imbued the air, he rose from his doorstep a changed man. Was it magic? No! not magic. The poor man had finally conquered his inner lassitude. For the first time in his life he felt the depth of his love for that scrap of ground lying bare under the sky, a scrap of ground upon which God's sunshine and generous rain fell neverthe-less. Suddenly, Gelp was seized by an overpowering desire for work, and with it came a great surge of strength, infusing his breast, his arms and shoulders, so that he could barely wait until the morning. That night his straw bed heaved under him like an antheap—like a veritable rack!

"What a waste of time and opportunity," he said, rebuking himself. "What wasted strength! Not just mine but the earth's too!"

Not in a year, not in two years had such a passion for work come over him, and all this time the earth had waited patiently for him . . . Waited for him, decking herself with wild flowers and herbs like a Gypsy girl, for Gelp had never clothed her with a golden robe of grain. Now he'd adorn her . . . Now he'd give her new life . . . Now he'd be her son. *Her* son! And she his birth mother!

The cockerels were already crowing when, exhausted by these thoughts, Gelp finally drifted off to sleep. He dreamed he was striding across the dark-blue heavens, harvesting the stars with a crescent moon for a scythe, and stacking them at God's feet . . . Aye! Such a golden dream he had!

At the first peep of dawn, Gelp took out the money he'd put away under the thatch and went to the wheelwright Adalbert who lived at the far end of the village. The road through the village was still quiet and deserted, but the old master was already seated astride his bench in front of his cottage, planing down a slender tree-trunk for a wagon shaft while whistling to his pet jackdaw. As soon as the bird saw Gelp, it called out: "Adalbert! Adalbert! Adalbert!" And turning its gray head, it cried out in a whistling treble: "Guest coming. Guest! Guest! Guest!"

"Praised be the Lord!" said Gelp, on coming up to the wheelwright.

"Forever and always!" replied Adalbert.

". . . ever and always!" repeated the jackdaw after him.

"Clever bird!" said Gelp in amazement. "Parish organist taught him, eh?"

"No," replied Adalbert. "Taught him myself!"

The old man was an orphan; his family and all his kin had died off, and having no one to talk to, he had at least his jackdaw to converse with.

"So what can I do for you?"

"I need a plow . . . a sturdy one!"

"Really! What are you aiming to plow? And who for?"

"Why, for myself! Me and my young'uns! I plan to sow wheat on that strip of ground they call 'the wasteland.'"

"You don't say!" said Adalbert in surprise. "For that you'd need a field-gun, not a plow. The land's overgrown . . . run wild . . . it'll be heavy going."

"Heavy . . . heavy . . . heavy!" repeated the daw, coughing and hacking like an old gaffer, for it could mimic such things too.

Gelp felt his heart sink. He felt the old lassitude descending on him, as if . . . But then right away he shook it off, saying:

"The plow must be strong, as the land is tough, the labor's tough, but then the laborer's tough, too! . . ."

And laughing out, he held up his veiny hands. He clenched his fists and stared at them with cheerful confidence.

"Well, then," said Adalbert. "I'll make you one!"

"Make you one . . . make you one! . . ." squawked the daw, flapping its wings with joy.

Gelp's eyes began to shine, and feeling a great surge of inner strength he proceeded quickly to explain his needs:

"Make me a plowshare, Adalbert, one that when I lean on it, it will cast the stones aside, left and right, wherever they crop up! Make me a coulter of the highest quality, one that shines like the sun, one that will cut deep into soil and allow the seed to settle in its very heart! Make me a strong moldboard, one that will lift and turn the clod, cut furrows from sunrise to sunset without stop, nice and even, as though it were treading a measure. Make me a pin for regulating the height, and a wheel, and a handle—a broad one, mind, sturdy and strong! And make sure you get the most suitable wood for it, not from the pine forest yonder but from a glade that the lark has sung to and pipes have played to, from a tree that's familiar with fields . . . Make me a plow like that!"

"Like that! Like that! Like that!" squawked the bird to high heaven, deafening Gelp.

Adalbert smiled benignly and nodded his hoary head.

"As you wish!" he said at last when the bird had quietened down. "It'll be as you wish! I make plows for the lazy and the hard-working. I make plows for squires and peasants! Ho! Ho! I make plows that slice through the ground as though it were butter, be it ever so hard and stony."

"Then make me one, dear Adalbert, and in good time!" said Gelp, untying a rag in which he'd wrapped his money. "I'll give you what I have. And make me a harrow, too."

"And why wouldn't I make one?" laughed out Adalbert. "I'll make a harrow with teeth sharper than a wolf's, one that'll groom the soil as smooth an old woman combs her flax. I've got it down to a fine art!"

"Well, then, God be with you!" said Gelp, who was raring to take to the axe and begin clearing his field. "I'll be back in a week."

"In a week, then," said Adalbert. "And God speed you in your work!"

"God speed! . . . God speed! . . . God speed!" squawked the daw to Gelp who was now striding briskly away as if he were ten years younger.

* * *

Villagers passing by the overgrown field would now stop and marvel. Who was this fellow spending every hour of the day chopping stumps, uprooting bushes, rolling away rocks, digging up blackthorn, pulling up wormwood and mullein, and excavating around the crab-trees? Who was this toiler with such fire in his eyes, dripping with sweat, as if he were wrestling a bear and never stopping to rest?

"Straighten up!" the peasants called out to him. "You'll end up with an arched back!"

"Who bends down to work is never bowed!" Gelp replied. "It's sloth and grief that bow a man down."

Young girls passing by took pity on him and entreated him with their thin little voices:

"Master Peter! Your brow's bedewed with sweat. Do rest a while!"

"Who bedews not his soil with sweat partakes not of its yield," Gelp replied.

Old women, heads wrapped in red kerchiefs, came by and watched his efforts.

"The poor fellow!" they said, shaking their heads. "All this grubbing for nothing! He'll never get to eat the grain he sows in that ground."

"If I don't, others will!" Gelp shouted back. "A man's here today, gone tomorrow, but the soil endures forever!"

Yet despite Gelp's gargantuan efforts, he would never have been able to move those great rocks or uproot even one of those stumps, if the Fair Folk hadn't been there helping him. He didn't see the little creatures, for they knew how to keep out of sight. Often, he quite surprised himself.

"Hey! Where does my strength come from?" he'd say, upon heaving up a huge stump sunk a fathom deep in the ground. "You'd need four stout fellows for a job like this!"

But what he didn't see was that there was a whole throng of Gnomes heaving on the stump beside him, digging out the soil around it, chopping at the roots with such gusto that the chips flew in all directions. For every blow of Gelp's axe, the Gnomes struck ten of their own, until, at last, the stump came out!

Gelp would move a boulder and be amazed at how easily it rolled.

"This isn't possible!" he thought. "A heavy rock like this, and see how lightly it trundles along." But he didn't see that there was a throng of Gnomes moving it with him. Such was the help he received, and so Gelp persevered with his work.

By the eighth day, no one would have recognized the former wasteland. From under the boulders, roots, shrubs, and rank herbage a new soil was laid bare to greet the morning sun. Huge, black resinous stumps stood stacked in front of his house for winter burning. Brushwood and blackthorn lay piled high on the balks. Here and yon, a hawthorn bush was left standing at the edges to mark the boundary, but otherwise the field stood entirely cleared, clean and even, the hillocks leveled out, the hollows filled in. And over this virgin soil soared a lark, pealing forth so loudly and gayly you'd think it was the morning reveille sounding on silver gusli strings.

Gelp wept with joy on bringing out his new—his very own!—plowshare. Doffing his cap, he knelt down and kissed the ground he'd restored to pristine condition; then thumping his chest twice with his fist he grasped the beam firmly with both hands, and sank the keen, wide shining share deep into the soil.

"Hey!" he cried. "Hey, thou field of mine!"

"Hey! Hey!" answered a cry from the nearby dell where the Fair Folk sat watching on the farther balk, singing and clapping their hands. King Glistel came out with his golden scepter to bless the new share, that it might bring grain out of the soil with joy and ease.

But that evening, when Gelp was returning home from his fragrant field, the memory of the dirt and disorder awaiting him in his hovel made him feel faint. Out here in the field it was clean and sweet-smelling. The sky above it was like a dark-blue lake. By day, the sun shone brightly over it; in the evening, the moon glided across it, striking sparks with her silver oar, and all around shone the stars. But in his wretched hovel everything was gray, sooty and dusty. Sweepings and heaps of refuse everywhere.

"Even the forest is lovelier," thought Gelp. "There the wild hops festoons the trees, while in the hut it's cobwebs hanging from corner to corner. The raven's black feathers glisten like water, while the shirts on our backs hang heavy with dirt. Even this lizard here has skin so clear and unblemished that the sun shines through it; meanwhile, my boys go about so scruffy and soiled you could plant turnips on them."

Weighed down by these thoughts and sighing deeply, he lowered his head and entered the hut. But what was this! Was this the same house? The brick chimney stood repointed, plastered over with clay, the cobwebs had been swept away, the bench, the table, the stools scrubbed clean, all the sweepings removed. The whole house stood brightened, transformed! The peasant rubbed his eyes, thinking all this would vanish when he looked again. But no! Here was same room, so spruce and fresh you could smell it.

"Who tidied up the place?" said Gelp.

"Why, Orphan Mary, and us too!" cried out little Daniel.

Gelp's heart melted like butter. It was as if better times had fallen upon him, as if something wondrous had compassed him and entered his soul through his eyes. He embraced the children tightly, and when he saw that the boys' hair had been neatly combed and their faces scrubbed clean, he shed a paternal tear on the three golden heads, and kissed them in turn.

It being suppertime, the swallow was just then returning to his nest to feed his babes. Three times he flew out and three times he returned, unable to recognize the hut, so much had it changed. But on observing all these changes, the bird burst into a joyful twitter:

> *Tweet! Tweet! Tweet!*
> *Sow your wheat!*
> *House keep neat!*
> *All is sweet!*
> *Tweet! Tweet! Tweet!*

As you can see, it was a very simple song, but the swallow's a rustic simpleton, incapable of singing otherwise. But then how blithely and gaily he twitters! How he raises a man's spirits! And so Gelp, too, felt strangely blithe and gay; and since he was all dusty and sweaty from toiling all day in the hot sun, he reached for a pail and went to the well where he washed his face and hands, shook the dust out of his hair, brushed off his clothes, and returning to the hut sat happily down to a bowl of boiled potatoes with the children.

All this was to become a regular habit with him. His boys, unused to seeing their father wash before supper and gaze on them so tenderly, marveled at the change they saw in him. Even the swallow was amazed.

"Easter must be coming!" Conrad conjectured seriously.

"Papa must be buying a suckling pig!" thought little Daniel.

For days afterwards the boys could be seen walking about, barefooted, tummies protruding, hands behind their backs, heads raised, their hair smoothed down with water. What could all this mean? they wondered; and padding about in this solemn manner, they longed for their Easter and suckling pig.

Before this, Gelp had never liked having the boys around him; he'd drive them away so as not to see them hungry and in need. But now he called them out into the field and had them sit near him on the balk, so as to hear the sound of their childish little voices. And wiping the sweat from his brow, he would smile and mutter to himself:

"It's hard for me, aye, but for you it'll be easier!"

\* \* \*

The day was coming to a close. The great ball of the sun was rolling gently down the western sky, aglow with roseate light. From the pine forest yonder advanced the moonlit night, trailing its silvery-misty robes. Here and yon in the dewy fields a corncrake rasped, a bittern boomed among the osiers by the forest, a flight of cranes cried languorously in the twilit sky, and the strong scent of grasses and herbs wafted over the earth. It was Midsummer's Night Eve, that strange and mysterious hour when people are able to understand the speech of beasts, birds, and every manner of herb.

This evening Gelp was plowing the last of his field. His brisk, eager cries could be heard all the way from the neighboring dell: "Gee-up! . . . Gee-up, my filly! . . . Whoa! . . . Giddup!" His boys, their flaxen heads leaning drowsily against each other, sat listening, watching from the dew-soaked balk beside a great heap of brushwood and blackthorn. The great expiring sun and the advancing night, heavy with dew, embraced them in a pair of silvery-gold wings and began rocking them to sleep. Suddenly, little Daniel stirred.

"The earth's talking . . ." he murmured slowly in a faint, sleepy voice.

"Don't be daft!" snorted Conrad indignantly. "The earth talking? Does it have a mouth to speak with?"

"You don't think so? . . ." said Daniel. "Then how does it ask Jesus for the rain or the sunshine? . . . The herbs and grasses speak . . ."

"Do you hear them?"

"Yes."

"What do they say?"

"Lots of things . . . Hush! Don't you hear them!"

Conrad strained his ears; indeed, there were murmurs and whispers coming from the pine woods and meadows— sounds that seemed to issue from thousands upon thousands of tiny, heaving breasts.

"Oh!" whispered Daniel again.

Conrad screwed up his eyes, thinking he'd hear better this way. But now these sounds were swelling and blending together, resolving themselves into ever more articulate words, seemingly distant yet so close you'd swear they were whispering in your soul. Then both boys heard a clear, song-like ringing sound—like the chiming of bluebells:

> Hush! . . . Hush! . . . Hush! . . .
> Ere Dawn's pink glow lights up the sky,
> Ere Morning's star peeps o'er the rim,
> We'll strew the earth with poppy seeds,
> The drowsy grass with silver dew;
> O'er lowly huts we'll scatter dreams—
> Soft dreams through silver sieves we'll sift!
> Hush! . . . Hush! . . . Hush! . . .

"You hear that?" whispered Conrad.

"Yes, and I'm afraid!" said little Daniel, and he clung still tighter to his brother.

Suddenly, the voices grew louder and clearer.

> Hush! . . . Hush! . . . Hush! . . .
> Through standing rye, through fragrant herb
> And scented grass, we whirl our dance.
> All through this night so rich in charms
> And spells we'll tread our lively dance;
> Aye, through the dandelion's cloud
> Of flying down we'll whirl all night!
> Hush! . . . Hush! . . . Hush! . . .

Suddenly, from under the stones, herbs and bushes there came a rustling sound then a noise like the thump of hundreds of tiny, hurrying feet. With bated breath the boys looked down, eyes rounding with wonder. The grass under an old decaying pear-tree beside them was swarming with colorfully clad little folk, their hands joined a merry dance.

"Gnomes! . . . The Little Folk!" whispered Conrad.

Just then the moon swung clear of the forest and lit up the entire glade with its silver luster.

"The King! . . ." cried Daniel in a stifled voice. "Oh! . . . The King! . . ." And he pointed his finger at the old field pear whence shone a brilliant white light. Blinded by the sudden brightness, Conrad could see nothing at first; then, as his eyes adjusted to the glare, he saw an exceedingly old king sitting in the cleft of the rotted tree. He was wearing a white robe, with a crown on his head and golden scepter in his hand. Conrad was about to cry out when sparks began shooting out of the great heap of brushwood and blackthorn that Gelp had cleared and piled on the balk. Up they flew like tiny golden bees; tiny snake-like tongues of fire licked the tinder below. At the same time the same quiet song resumed:

> Hush! . . . Hush! . . . Hush! . . .
> Oh, hear the crackling of the wood!
> The snapping of the golden sparks!
> Midsummer's fire we light for you—
> How merrily it flames and flares!
> How bright the glow it casts about!
> How high leap up the merry flames!
> Hush! . . . Hush! . . . Hush! . . .

And as if in answer to the song, the pile of brushwood and blackthorn burst into bright flames, and in their brilliant light the Gnomes could be seen dancing. Faster and faster they whirled, ever lighter, ever airier, so that to look at them made one's head spin.

"Heavens! . . . Papa!' cried Conrad in sudden terror. "Papa! Come and see! The Gnomes are dancing!"

"The King . . . the King!" whispered Daniel, staring spellbound at the pear-tree. And trembling with fear and the cold dew, he covered his head with his thin little arms, even as a drowsy bird covers its head with its wings.

But Gelp saw and heard nothing. The sweat was cooling on his back, his aching shoulders throbbed, and his eyes burned with an immense, quiet joy. Having finished plowing the last of the field, he drove his share into the balk. There, removing his cap, he gazed up at the wide moonlit sky and spoke in a strong voice:

"Thank you, Lord, for helping me in this labor—Amen!"

And seizing his nag by the bridle, he led it briskly over to where his boys were sitting. Despite all his exertions, he strode like one after a delicious rest, blithe and light of step, the brightness and the calm of the night permeating him to the very bones. And all around he could hear sounds, soft, muted sounds, as if coming from an invisible choir of violins.

> *Hush! . . . Hush! . . . Hush!*
> *The plowman's toil is done at last;*
> *Now shall we dance till morning breaks,*
> *Till the last bright spark dims and dies*
> *And Dawn's soft hand bestrews the sky*
> *With roses; aye, now shall we dance*
> *All night around the blazing fire!*
> *Hush! . . . Hush! . . . Hush!*

Listening as one entranced, Gelp cast his gaze over his plowed field shining in the silver moonlight. Before him, at his very feet, fell his short shadow. There it lay, distinctly outlined on the ground. He looked at it once, looked again, then let out a heavy sigh. Alas, was this shadow not like the dark fate that accompanied him wherever he went? He hung his head and fell into a deep funk; the airy music stopped sounding in his ears. So, what now that his field was plowed and the soil lay prepared? . . . How was he to sow it when he had no seed, and nothing to buy it with? What he'd earned at the sawmill and saved up for these better times had all been spent on the plow, the harrow, the axe, his food—this despite the tight grip he exerted on the rag containing his pennies, a grip so tight it made the rag scrunch in his hand! But what good was this crimping and scrimping when he needed to pay the blacksmith, or buy salt? . . . Only the day before he'd spent the last groat . . . So what now? . . . What to do about the soil that needed to be sown?

And plunged in this funk, Gelp returned to his hut, his shadow following him all the way. He passed the fence. The shadow followed him. He reached his door. Still the shadow followed. It even fell on the doorstep; who knows, perhaps it even slipped into the hut, but Gelp no longer saw it. Tossing his cap on the table, he sat down heavily on the bench. He was still brooding when the door suddenly creaked open, and in skipped little Mary, returning from a distant errand.

# 10

# A Thief in the Night

Every day from the first flush of dawn, the pounding of threshing flails could be heard throughout the village. Now they fell singly: *Thump, thump!* . . . now in pairs: *Thumpity, thump! Thumpity, thump!* . . . now in threes: *Thump, thumpity, thump! Thump, thumpity, thump!* . . . then in fours: *Thumpity, thumpity, thump, thump! Thumpity, thumpity, thump, thump!* Faster and harder they fell until their echoes sprang back from the forest yonder. Such was the villagers' haste to catch the sowing season in good time.

Gelp alone stood idle-handed. He had no grain crop to thresh. Sad and listless, he trudged back and forth, from his hut to his field then from his field to his hut, brooding, thinking where he might find grain for sowing. Meanwhile, the field, its furrows running straight and even under the silent sky, was crying for grain. The sun was warming it, the dew refreshing it. From dawn to dusk the lark—songster of the plowed field—soared above it, pealing forth its bright song:

> *God grant it! God grant it!*
> *A field of golden shocks,*
> *Each shock a dozen sheaves,*

> *Each sheaf replete with grain,*
> *Each grain its weight in gold.*
> *God grant it! God grant it!*

Hearing the song, Gelp shook his head and sighed. "O earth! O earth!" he muttered. "I've plowed you. I've harrowed you, but all I've sown are tears!"

Meanwhile, in the village the threshing went on apace: *Thump, thump! Thumpity thump!* The flailers beat the golden sheaves, extracting the golden grain. Those who beat harder sent the grain flying beyond the threshing floor to the very doors of the open barn. Like golden sparks they flew, as when the smith beats iron on the anvil. At the barn doors there reigned a mighty commotion. Throngs of sparrows were dropping down from the nearby poplars, chirping, pecking, arguing and fighting over the scattered grain, then at the slightest untoward disturbance—frr! . . . fluttering back to the trees, as if swept up by the wind.

"Why are the birds so noisy today?" wondered the peasants. "Is it going to rain? Is it the weather?"

But what they didn't see was that among the sparrows there was a throng of Gnomes gathering up the scattered grains. For every grain a sparrow seized, a Gnome picked up ten. How they bustled! The sparrows hopped madly around the bobbing red hoods, ruffling their feathers, chirping and squawking. But the Gnomes, not in the least frightened by these squawkers, went calmly among them, gathering the choicest grains into little sacks or the upturned borders of their cloaks.

"Here, you sparrows, these cracked grains you're free to take. But the whole and unblemished ones, the ones that shine like gold—those are for sowing! One grain seed sown in the ground yields a hundredfold. From these the poor wight makes his bread and feeds his tots. Then you, too, shall partake of the bounty."

So spoke the Gnomes as they gathered up the grain. But their words were lost on the feathered throng. After all, birds are birds! Birds do not fret about tomorrow; they neither sow nor reap, and yet they thrive. Today their crops are full, they lift their heads and sing. Tomorrow comes—again they lift their heads and sing blithely, trusting in what the day will bring.

Meanwhile, the villagers threshed, and every day the Gnomes collected the choicest grains. What they gathered during the day they carried off and laid up in store underground. The storage place was dry, vaulted by the great roots of an excellently chosen oak-tree and lined inside with birch bark so that the entire chamber shone like silver. There was a moss-lined opening above for the air to pass through, and another opening in the side to enter in by. On the floor lay a great heap of the choicest golden grain—a good three bushels! Of course, such rich bounty could not be left untended and unguarded. Every day one of the Gnomes turned the grain with a linden-wood spade, spread it out to dry, and let the sun in through the opening. When night came, he swept the grain back into a heap with a whiskbroom, closed the upper opening to prevent the damp air from entering, then lying down by the entrance he'd go to sleep.

Now one night Willowkin, whose turn it was to mind the grain, noticed that the pile had shrunk in size. "Hmm, maybe it's settled a bit!" he thought. And so passed the night. The next night the pile seemed to have sunk even lower. "Hmm!" thought Bluebonnet who was on duty that night. "Perhaps it's dried a bit!" But on the third night, the pile had fallen so low that Maribeetle, whose turn it was then, seized his head in his hands and ran to alert the others. No doubt about it! Someone was stealing the grain. The Gnomes came running in a body to have a look. What mischief was this? Why, not even half of the original pile left! But no use moaning, something had to be done.

"Gracious King!" cried the Gnomes. "A thief s raiding our grain! What are we to do?"

"You'll have to catch him!"

"But Your Majesty!" they cried. "The thief's like the wind in the field. He can take a hundred paths. Who's going to catch him?"

"I shall give you my signet ring and sealing wax," King Glistel replied. "Place a seal over every chink you find; this way you'll know by which of these hundred paths our thief goes in and out."

The Gnomes took the royal signet and wax; they stuffed the chinks with silver moss, barred them with trellises of reeds, knotted up the longest grass, sealed the knots with wax and applied the seal, then placing guards at the entrance they waited.

Night came. A profound silence! You could have heard a poppy seed drop. Not a tree-leaf stirred. Breathless over the earth hung the dark sky, a-gleam with as many stars as grains of sand by the seashore.

Standing guard that night were the twin brothers, Muckle and Ruckle, whom King Glistel had appointed police officers of the court. He'd outfitted them splendidly with bluebell heads for helmets, and swords from the sword-lily[1] whose fiery flower shoots up from her long sword-like leaves like a hussar's red-pennoned lance. Muckle stood stiffly at attention as if he'd swallowed a stick. Straight as a ramrod stood Ruckle. Only their eyeballs moved sharply from side to side.

Meanwhile, all of Nightingale Dell slept: the blue stream, the reeds, the flies and birds, the choirs of frogs, the water lilies, and the old oak under which Muckle and Ruckle stood guard. At the first peep of dawn, the Gnomes sprang out of bed and ran down in a body to the vault. There stood the guards, just as they'd been stationed, there lay the seals—unbroken, but to their utter amazement the vault was now almost empty. Barely enough grain to cover the floor! The Gnomes stood aghast. What kind of thief could have got in and left without breaking the seals? They stared at each other in silence; no one could think of a word to say. At last the King broke the silence.

"If neither my signet ring nor my guards succeeded in protecting the grain, then nothing will!"

But then Peterkin, who always had a lively thought in his head, called out from the throng:

"What will you give me, Gracious King, if I catch the thief?"

"A voice on his behalf when the culprit stands arraigned before the court!" replied the King.

"What?" cried Peterkin. "A voice for a thief? Why, I shouldn't lift a finger to save him, hangman or no! I'd sooner have Sarabanda's musical score, since it's of no use to Half-Lord who has lost his voice."

---

1 The gladiolus flower.

"So let it be!" said the King, waving his scepter, for so marvelously had the Maestro's song been inscribed on the leaves of the field roses and butterflies' wings (not in ink but in Maytime's purest dew!) that the King had had it deposited in his treasury along with the rest of his precious jewels. Peterkin leapt almost an ell high with joy, then squeezing the King's knee leapt up again and sped off like the wind across the field into the dark forest.

\* \* \*

Dawn was breaking and the birds were starting to peep in the forest when Peterkin found himself before the low door of the old crone's hut. The one-room dwelling was dreadfully poor and but for the stove, a small table and tattered daybed, quite bare. But then there were herbs galore! Herbs hanging from the rafters, on the walls, herbs strewn over the earthen floor, herbs in baskets or wrapped in pieces of cloth, in small bundles or entire sheaves—nothing but herbs! The stifling blend of scents—of mint, thyme, lavender, chamomile, balm, and a thousand others—filled the hut. One might have suffocated from all these strong exhalations if not for the opening in the thatch that looked out on a blue sky blocked from view only by the wings of a tawny owl.

The woman sat by the stove, treadling on a spinning wheel, singing old ditties. A golden spindle whirred silently in her hand.

"Greetings, Old Dame!" said Peterkin from the threshold.

Raising her head, the woman put her hand to her eyes and stared at him until she recognized the Gnome as the one who flown to her house for a golden needle.

"Ah, greetings, greetings!" she replied. "Come right in! What is your need today?"

Peterkin walked in, bowed low before her, and kissed her wrinkled hand.

"I need your advice. A thief is stealing our goods, and we can't catch him. Such a misfortune!"

Listening intently, the old woman took her foot off the treadle, let the golden spindle fall to the floor, and with the golden yarn still in her fingers sat silent, shaking her hoary head, deep in thought.

"And what is the thief stealing?" she said at last.

"He's stealing our grain," said Peterkin with great indignation. "The grain we stored for sowing. The scoundrel!"

"Then cast some pearls in with the grain!"

"What!" cried Peterkin. "Pearls? A thief steals our grain, and you say throw in pearls as well? Has age muddled your mind, Old Mother?"

But the crone had already picked up the golden spindle, set the spinning wheel in motion, and resumed running the golden yarn through her fingers.

"Cast pearls in with the grain," she repeated and began humming her old ditty again in a soft, shaky voice, as if Peterkin were not there.

"Grandmother!" he cried out. "I came to you as I'd go to my own mother, my birth mother. I didn't go to the Day, or the Night, or the Sun, or the Moon, but to you, since I know you are wise and your wisdom is the gleaning of many days and many nights, of many risings and settings of the sun and moon. And this is how you receive me? This is the advice you give me? Bless you, Old Mother, but I can see I've deceived myself."

Great was the sorrow in his voice, great the rancor in his heart. He started toward the door, but just as he reached it, the crone stopped singing and called out to him:

"Pearls! . . . Give him pearls! Cast pearls in with the grain! . . ."

"I see! . . . Right!" muttered Peterkin, and he went on his way, regretting the time and effort he'd wasted.

But the sound of the old woman's voice pursued him. Louder and stronger it grew, diffusing through the air in ever-widening circles and so filling it that even though Peterkin was now a long way off, it flew after him, swept over and by him, constantly calling:

"Pearls . . . Give him pearls! . . . Pearls!"

The great power of that voice caused Peterkin to stop and wonder. Could that voice be expressing some profound truth?

"Hmm!" he said to himself. "Perhaps the crone's got something there? Perhaps that's what we need to do?" And he began to ponder the matter.

"What will be will be," he said at last, "but hanging the scoundrel is out of the question!"

And since he was a venturesome little Gnome, always ready to try something new, he ran back home and went before the King.

"Your Majesty!" he said. "How many pearls would you entrust me with, if I stood guard tonight?"

"Who entrusts one, entrusts them all!" replied the King. "But I value your loyalty more than I do pearls."

"Graciously spoken, O King! Entrust me with a handful of pearls, and if I'm to catch this thief, I shall."

"Then go, take them!" said the King.

And right away Glistel ordered his treasurer to give Peterkin a generous handful of pearls, whereupon the sprightly Gnome wiped away a tear or two (for he had soft heart), squeezed the King's knee, thanked him, then bursting into a merry laugh went to the treasury to collect his pearls. From there he proceeded directly down to the vault, for dusk was gathering even now. The Gnomes followed him in a body and watched him with keen interest.

"In your name, Old Mother! May your wisdom hold true!" said Peterkin, scattering the pearls over the grain. Then turning to his comrades he added, "No need for guards or sealing wax tonight! Muckle! Ruckle! Off to bed with you, my friends! I'm standing watch tonight."

And without further ado, he lay down on a mound, pillowed his head on a stone, and with a drowsy eye watched his comrades depart. A light wind was blowing from the east, causing the long grass outside to rustle softly as though someone were whispering and murmuring there. But Peterkin paid no attention to these sounds; exhausted by the day's arduous trek, he fell into a deep slumber and slept soundly until daybreak.

Upon waking up, he looked around, and—would you believe it!—before his very feet lay a path of pearls that led out of the vault and into the dell in the direction of Gelp's field. At once he raised the alarm, and began to follow the trail; the roused Gnomes ran in a body behind him. On he ran, now stopping in his tracks and kneeling down, now starting up again. Every dozen paces or so he came upon a gleaming pearl, as if someone had scooped it up along with the grain then stopped to discard it as being of no use to him, and made off again with just the grain.

The rat gave out a loud squeak and struggled to break free, but now the court police had him firmly in their grasp.

"Oh, wise, wise Old Mother!" thought Peterkin as he emerged from the dell and halted at the edge of Gelp's field. Looking out, he saw a last pearl lying at the bottom of a deep furrow; beside it rose a small mound of freshly stirred soil, and right by it was a little hole! Peterkin bent down and began grubbing in the mound. Two or three more satin pearls came rolling out before his eyes! He yelled out to his companions and together they dug until they unearthed a large cellar containing nearly all of the stolen grain; and there, huddled beside the pile of grain, crouched a field rat and his family.

"Got you!" cried Peterkin, seizing the offender by the neck. "Muckle! Ruckle! Come quick, both of you!"

The terrified rat gave out a loud squeak and struggled to break free, but now the court police had firmly in their grasp and he was forced to come quietly. Great was the Gnomes' triumph! With shouts and songs they returned from their expedition, leading their prisoner and bearing the stolen grain in sacks to its former place of storage.

\* \* \*

The page Tubkin was holding up the train of the King's purple robe; the golden crown shone on the royal head, and the diamond ball of His Majesty's scepter scattered beams like the rising sun. Before the tribunal bench stood State Prosecutor Sharpeye; beside him, in dress uniform, stood Muckle and Ruckle, and at a respectable distance around them crowded the Gnomes, all eyes fixed on the defendant. Clad in a wretched shirt, ashen-faced, the accused stood cowering in the dock, his forepaws bound tightly behind his back. He was trembling violently and barely able to support himself on his legs, as if in a fever.

The silver-tongued Prosecutor, his voice now grown hoarse and wheezy, was summing up the charges against him. He demanded the harshest punishment: at the very least hanging the felon from the highest bough of the oak-tree along with full damages and recompense for the cost of the process.

The King raised his scepter and addressed the accused:

"What is your name, wretched creature?"

The rat turned deathly pale and swayed on his legs. Muckle had to prod him with his truncheon.

"Nibbles . . . at your service!" replied the rat in a bare whisper.

"Why did you steal the grain?" said the King.

"I was hungry . . . in desperate need . . . my children were starving . . ."

"But does hunger give you the right to steal another's goods?"

"No, Gracious King!" said Nibbles, quaking in his boots.

"Then what have you to say for yourself?"

"Nothing . . . except hunger . . . hunger . . . terrible hunger . . ."

"But even in the greatest hunger you couldn't have eaten that amount of grain. One tenth would have been enough for you and your children."

"I feared the winter . . . Gracious King! . . . Winter is harsh and terribly long . . . Half of my children died last winter. Oh, how they suffered! . . . The youngest . . . my youngest child, O King, was dying of hunger before my eyes . . . Six days and six nights I watched him die . . . and I lived . . . lived! . . and I couldn't die in his stead . . . I couldn't!"

The King turned his venerable face away; pity stood writ upon it, and a silent sobbing could be heard from among the Gnomes. It was Peterkin weeping.

Nibbles went on:

"After the youngest, it was the eldest . . . My eldest son, O King . . . dying before my eyes . . . Ten days and ten nights it took for him to die . . . and I watched . . . and I couldn't die in his stead, though I was dying with him!"

The King furrowed his brow to stem the tears starting from his eyes, and a deep sigh could be heard coming from among the Gnomes. Peterkin was sobbing loudly.

Nibbles went on:

"And then it was my third . . . My third son, O King, was dying of hunger . . . and I watched . . . Before my very eyes my son was dying of hunger . . . And I couldn't die!"

And suddenly the rat began to shake all over and, closing his eyes, he whispered in a lifeless voice, "Hunger . . . hunger . . . hunger . . ."

Then King Glistel raised his scepter and spoke forth:

"I must be severe, since you are sorely to blame. The grain you stole was intended for sowing—sowing for an unfortunate like you, who also has starving children. Let justice then be served."

"Death! Death to the felon!" cried Sharpeye.

"Death!" cried Muckle and Ruckle grimly after him.

Thunderstruck and trembling violently, Nibbles looked around him.

The King turned away. He was about to leave the hall when, suddenly, Peterkin leapt out from the throng and cast himself at his feet.

"I wish to be heard!" he cried out. "A voice for the accused, Gracious King! You promised me a voice. A voice! I want a voice! . . ."

"Then you have it!" said the King, and leaning down from his dais he tapped him gently with his scepter.

"Forgive him! Forgive him, Gracious King!" cried Peterkin, sobbing. "Forgive him! Say you'll forgive him, O King! Say it! It will be my song! My finest song! My one and only! I wish no other! None! . . ."

Seeing such a violent outburst of grief from his cherished servant, the old King wept.

"You have conquered me, dear Peterkin!" he said. "You have tempered my justice with mercy. Let it be as you wish!"

And raising his scepter, he declared:

"Release the poor wretch and feed his children! Henceforth they shall eat of the bread from my table. Now convey the grain to the plowman and the field that cries to be sown."

\* \* \*

The orphan girl was up to her elbows in work, cleaning up Gelp's hut as best she could. Now and then, she looked into the overgrown garden. What an eyesore it was! "If only I had some hemp," she thought. "What a delight it would be: clearing it, drying it, breaking it, then on long winter evenings spinning it into golden thread!" She recalled her mother sitting down at such work and the beautiful songs she'd sing while so engaged. "And then a few rows of cabbages!" she thought. "The soil's black and fertile. Why, their heads would be big as pumpkins!" And Little Orphan Mary began to think how she might apply herself to the garden. "Come springtime, I'll dig up the garden . . . but can a little girl do it all on her own?" Suddenly, she clapped her hands. Why, she had ready workers in Conrad and little Daniel!

But it wasn't only the thought of the neglected garden that agitated Mary. More and more often she was thinking about her little geese, about the knoll on the sunlit pasture with its yellow flowers, and her dog Oscar who'd sit there at her side, tearing away now and then, and barking loudly whenever the geese strayed too close to the forest.

* * *

One evening, after finishing her household chores, Mary decided to walk to the nearby common. Upon arriving there, she gazed out. Suddenly, she spotted what looked like a pointy red hood moving quickly through the tall grass. "Why, it's Spratkin!" she cried; and with a pounding heart she tore off after him; it was a wonder her heart didn't shatter that meager little breast of hers! On she ran, but the little hood was drawing farther and farther away; now it had vanished into a thicket. She plunged in after it. She wanted so much to see the Gnome and ask him things. What about, exactly, she didn't yet know, but if only she could catch him and thank him for everything, for her geese that were alive, for her little corner in Gelp's hut, for Conrad and Daniel, who were like brothers to her . . . On she plunged through the dense shrubbery as fast as it would allow her. At last, the hood vanished from sight and did not reappear. Mary stopped and looked about her. Where had she got to? She was coming to the end of the thicket, and the evening sun could be seen glowing through it. Beyond the thicket stood the forest—the forest she knew so well. She ran on all the way to the far end of Famine Hamlet where she used to live. From there she decided to venture still farther, to the old pasture ground, where she might catch a glimpse of her white and brindled geese and dear little Oscar? And there, indeed, drawing up behind a large shrub near the familiar knoll, she spied her geese calmly nibbling on the grass; there was her faithful Oscar running around them. In the adjacent cornfield stood a young girl. It was the new gooseherd. Stooping and rising, she was picking late poppies, cornflowers and cockles for a garland. And so Mary watched from her point of espial.

At last, the sun went down; the gooseherd gathered the flock and, with Oscar's help, drove them home, the dog constantly yapping at the white goose. Even under Mary's care it would lag behind the rest, but when the girl swished her willow branch at her, the bird scooted forward to join the gander at the head of the flock.

The little herd disappeared behind a hill, and Mary was left standing alone behind the shrub. Unable to catch Spratkin, she had reckoned at least on greeting Oscar and the geese; in the event, they'd all left, and she hadn't greeted them. The truth is that Mary was afraid of the new gooseherd. Such a timid thing she was! But now that she'd ventured this far, she risked remaining here a while longer. And parting the shrubbery with her hands . . . Heavens! What was this?! On the ground before her lay a dead hamster, and a few yards away from it—the lifeless body of Greasy Tod! Both animals had torn fur and were covered with gory wounds.

Mary wrung her hands and gaped in amazement. The sight of Greasy Tod filled her with dread. But the hamster! Could this be *her* little hamster? She ran to its burrow and cleared the stalks that lay trampled around it. Tufts of the hamster's fawn fur and the fox's red pelt clung to the stalks; drops of congealed blood hung like coral on the leaves; the soil around the entrance to the burrow lay disturbed, dug up with claws.

"Poor little thing!" cried Mary, aghast.

Aye, poor thing, indeed! Greasy Tod had kept his promise. He'd wreaked his grim vengeance on the little beast. But then wasn't the hamster also to blame? Why had he turned a blind eye to the fox creeping up on the geese? Why hadn't he warned the gooseherd, or Oscar, at least? The geese would have suffered no misfortune, and the fox would have had to have shown a clean pair of heels. And now here the little animal lay lifeless. Hapless hamster! By thinking only of your needs, you doomed yourself!

Looking around, Mary saw a patch of flattened grass a few feet from the burrow. Evidently, Greasy Tod had been lying in ambush there. He must have pounced on the hamster, but in so doing disturbed the dry stalks and startled the animal, who retreated into his burrow. The bandit pursued him. Two scrapes of his powerful paws and he was inside the burrow; and a terrible battle broke out! The hamster dealt him a deep, mortal wound before finally succumbing to the much bigger animal, who then dragged him away into the bushes. The fox would have taken him to his den, but evidently his own life's blood had been flowing out of him.

Poor little hamster! If something could have cheered him in that last hour of his life, it would have been the extraordinary valor he'd shown in this mortal struggle with the cruel beast. To leap, heedless of the outcome, at the throat of such an animal— now that took courage! He perished, but so did his foe, despite his greater size and strength. And so, redeeming by his death his previous indifference to the common weal, a tiny hamster had rid the whole district of a cruel and depraved marauder!

Meanwhile, Mary stood before the dead hamster. She gazed at its torn fur, at those once keen, now lifeless eyes, at those motionless yet still forbidding little whiskers that used to twitch so cheerfully. Pity and sorrow so seized Mary's heart that a flood of silver tears spilled from under her lowered eyelashes and streamed down her pale cheeks. Sobbing bitterly, she knelt down beside the animal and spoke to it in a sweet voice, as though it could still hear her.

"Fear not, fear not, poor little thing. I won't leave you here next to this loathsome fox, this nasty bandit. I'll take you with me, my dear! . . . I'll bury you . . . yes! Nice and deep, in Gelp's garden, under the great oak-tree there. I'll strew the bottom with leaves . . . cover you nicely with more leaves. . . .There you'll rest peacefully. . . . No, I shan't leave you here! I'll have close by me at least one little friend from the old days."

At once she began gathering up evergreen sprays. Laying them over the hamster, she took the resin-scented little bundle into her apron, turned and hastened back to Gelp's hut.

Now, if she had only cast her eye on a nearby clump of burdocks, she would have seen, though there was not the slightest breath of wind, those large round leaves swaying, and something like a red flame flickering among them. As it was, scarcely did she turn back toward Gelp's hut when the leaves parted, and out crept a tiny Gnome. It was Peterkin.

"Did she take it?" he whispered.

"She did!" answered another soft voice from among a clump of stalks beside the hamster's burrow. And just as stealthily as Peterkin before him, Spratkin emerged.

He put his finger to his lips, but Peterkin, who was lively by nature and unable to restrain himself, began jumping about and shouting gleefully:

"So we did it! We did it!"

"Silence, you fool!" hissed Spratkin, seizing him by the arm. "You're raising such a racket, you'd think we were alone! She might hear us yet . . ."

"Hear us? How? Our evening crickets sing so loud they'd drown anything out! But tell me again, did we succeed? Did we?"

"What was not to succeed! She's such a sweet soul—the soul of kindness."

"Isn't she so! . . . Sweeter than honey! It wouldn't have been so easy with someone else."

"But those promptings of yours about the oak and the burial! You were so loud I was afraid she'd peek into the burdocks!"

"That's the way I am!" said Peterkin. "Straight from the shoulder! What will be will be. As you see, she didn't notice."

"Oh, my aching knees!" groaned Spratkin. "Kneeling here among these stalks since morning, keeping the ants off the hamster so Mary wouldn't mind touching it."

"And I—said Peterkin—thought I'd break a leg running so fast to lead her to this spot. She even thought I was you, since with everything else I'd donned my hood and borrowed Bluebonnet's tobacco pipe, to look more like you. Ooh! And when I dived into the burdocks, I thought I'd scream…Imagine! The place was full of nettles! If it wasn't for His Majesty, I'd have leapt out there and then…But the King is of the firm mind that the grain should come to Gelp by way of the waif…that he might take her under his roof for good…"

"Aye, our gracious King!" said Spratkin approvingly.

"Right! Now let's go after her. Stealthfully does it!"

"Know what, Peterkin? Better take those boots off. They creak terribly…"

"Me? Take off my boots! Whatever next! Maybe you don't mind going about barefoot. You'd have got used to it at that woman's whose babe you changed places with. But me? The King's invested courtier? What an idea!…"

"Then don't if you won't, but let's be off, and don't creak!"

"Me? Creak?…Right, let's go!"

And taking each other by the hand, they began to follow the orphan girl, Peterkin walking on the toes of his tall red boots that creaked like an ungreased cart, and Spratkin flapping his oversized clogs that kept parting company with his feet.

* * *

Meanwhile, the moon stood high in the sky, silvering the path with her luster. Along this path, all white in the brilliance, walked Mary, her head upraised, her thin little hands holding tightly to the borders of her apron with its little bundle wrapped in evergreen sprays. She walked quickly, for she still had chores to do at home and prepare for the night. As she went, she debated with herself whether she should tell

Conrad and Daniel about the hamster. But even as she so debated, something nearby whispered in her ear:

"No, no! Don't tell the boys! First bury the hamster! True, they're good little boys, but they're given to pranks. Better not tell them, no!"

Imagining these to be her own thoughts, Mary hastened her steps, not noticing that beside her own shadow which the moonlight was casting on the path, there glided another tiny shadow. It was Peterkin's. He was very concerned that Mary should bury the hamster herself, and it was he that had prompted her so. Delighted to have accomplished the task, he made two great leaps into the air and returning to Spratkin's side pulled his companion's hood right over his head.

"What's the matter with you today?" snapped Spratkin.

"Oh, I'm so glad! So glad the King will be happy. If we didn't have to follow the girl, I'd be turning somersaults here till morning!"

"Whatever for?"

"What do you mean, whatever for? Don't you know that when Gnomes turn somersaults in the moonlight, the village women start squabbling among themselves."

"Well? What of it?"

"Nothing, Let them squabble! Tomorrow's Saturday. They'll be making butter, and when a woman's cross, she'll churn the butter faster. You'll see how rich the buttermilk will be!"

"You talk such nonsense!"

"Nonsense? Think what you're saying! Buttermilk, nonsense?"

"Listen, Peterkin," said Spratkin, his hand on his companion's shoulder. "There's no time to lose. See? We're approaching Gelp's hut. Did you manage to find a mattock to place under the oak-tree?"

"No bother at all! There was one in the hut by the door."

"That's good! . . . Look! She's going right up to the oak . . . Sweet little thing!"

Indeed, Mary was making straight for the oak that was rustling softly and tenderly, as though speaking words. Upon reaching it, the girl began to look for a stick with which to delve a little grave. Suddenly, she noticed Gelp's mattock leaning against the oak.

"Thank you, dear Lord!" she whispered. "You've provided me with a mattock . . . Now I'll be able to dig a nice big hole!"

At once she lay the hamster on the grass and began swinging the mattock. She struck once, then again, marveling at how easily the delving went. The mattock was light as a feather, the soil crumbly, as if recently stirred.

"How much stronger I've grown living on Gelp's bread," she marveled with a smile. "I didn't have half—no, not a quarter—of this strength when I tended the geese."

She fell silent, then sighing softly said: "Oh, how will I, an orphan, repay him for his kindness? . . . but God will repay him."

Just as she was muttering these words, her mattock broke through the thin layer of topsoil, and a deep hole opened up beneath it; the girl barely prevented the tool from falling inside.

"Gracious!" she said. "Don't these oak roots make space for themselves in the soil! Well, let them! There'll be plenty of room for my hamster."

Suddenly the moon shone through the boughs above and lit up the base of the tree. Mary reached for a twig, and upon thrusting it deep into the hole felt some loose particles fall into her hand. She drew it out, looked at it— why, it was wheat! Golden kernels of wheat! She reached in again and drew out a handful of grain—grain such as you'd find in a strapping peasant's granary! Nothing but grain wherever her hand groped . . . The moon was shining brighter and brighter, the world grew whiter, and from the grain came a luster such as only fairy tales describe; and all the while the oak whispered softly and tenderly, "God will return the kindness, little waif!"

"Heavens! Heavens!" said Mary in astonishment, and with a loud cry she leapt up and ran as fast she could to Gelp's hut. She burst in through the door, her heart beating like a bird in her breast. Inside she found Gelp sitting on a stool by the stove, his head downcast, his gnarled fingers buried in his tangled hair.

"Master! . . . Papa!" she cried in a breathless voice, tears of joy spilling like pearls from her eyes.

But Gelp was so preoccupied with thoughts of grain he hadn't heard the creaking of the door.

"Papa!" she repeated, running up to him and pulling on his sleeve. "We have wheat!"

He looked wild-eyed at her, not understanding what she was saying. It must have been a dream, he thought; she'd only imagined it. But the orphan persisted; she wouldn't be silenced.

"We have wheat, Papa! Lots of wheat! . . . "

Gelp screwed up his eyes; the blue veins bulged across his brow.

"What are you saying? What are you saying, girl?" he said, gripping and raising her little arm.

"Just that! . . ." said Mary under his arm, her eyes beaming like candles. "I'm saying, Papa, that we have wheat for sowing."

Gelp sprang from the stool and seized his cap. "What? . . . Where? Where is this wheat of yours?" His hands shook, his legs trembled, and his voice caught in his throat so that he couldn't speak for joy.

"Merciful Jesus! Where? Where? . . ."

"Over there, under the oak! Under our very own oak-tree!" cried Mary excitedly. "Bring a bedsheet or a sack, because it's a giant pile!"

"Jesu! Sweet Jesu!" cried Gelp, reaching for a sack on the stove-shelf.

"Giant pile, you say . . . God bless you, little waif! Such happiness you bring me. It's as if you were my own . . . my very own child."

But Mary was already standing at the door.

"Let's go, Papa! Quickly! While the moon still shines . . ."

And off they sped.

# 11

# Half-Lord's Alms

_____

Since the day Fiddle-Fuddle had unwittingly helped Greasy
Tod to carry out his dastardly crime, he had been biding in
the den, waiting impatiently for him to return. Normally, the
fox left his earth in the evening and returned at dawn, with
this notable difference that upon leaving it he took the narrow underground passage that led toward the village, but
upon returning, gorged and bloated, he entered by the wider
entrance from the side of the forest. Once home, he would
cast himself down and sleep soundly all day until dusk. The
Gnome wondered about these nightly expeditions of his, but
being a polite guest, he was loath to pry. One day Greasy Tod
confided in the Gnome himself:

"You see before you, sir, the most wretched, four-legged
beast ever to walk this earth! My mother was a somnambulist;
it was from her I inherited this disposition! What I didn't
have to pay those doctors, those quacks and shysters! What
powders, potions, balms, and pills didn't they prescribe! I
spent half my fortune on them. It's enough to tell you, sir, that
those prescriptions alone heated my house for three winters,
and despite the fierce frost outside, it was toasty warm inside!
And all for naught! The moon has only to peep out in the east

and I'm driven to go prowling about like a cat on the rooftops. I even tried to tie my tail to the peg you see fixed there to the wall, but to no avail. When the rope jerked me back, the most beautiful part of my brush was left attached to the peg, and I found myself standing at the threshold. Here, sir, have a look! I still bear the traces of that incident! There's rumors circulating that it was the blacksmith's dogs that tore out part of my tail, which, of course, is pure libel and outright slander! And so I've resigned myself to my fate. So much is sleepwalking part of my nature that whether there's a moon out or not, I feel compelled to leave my den the moment it grows dark. Indeed, the darker it is, the more strongly I'm driven out toward the village. Sometimes the night is so black the darkness fairly hums, and I, wretched beast that I am, gravitate to where there's a henhouse or goose-pen. It's only the sounds of clucking hens, crowing roosters—to say nothing of gaggling geese—that give me a measure of solace! Hah! The will of Heaven!"

Here Greasy Tod sighed so mightily that his whiskers stood up like panicles under his nose, whereupon he lay down and fell asleep, snoring loudly—licking his chops in his dreams.

But today Fiddle-Fuddle was especially anxious. Morning passed, the noon hour passed, and still the fox hadn't returned. Twice the learned chronicler went outside to have a look. Before him, as far as the eye could see, stretched the forest, its trees conversing mysteriously, their crowns swaying in the breeze. Lower down, squirrels scampered over the boughs of the oaks and beeches, and, lower still, whispered the ferns, mosses, and clustering guelder roses; but apart from these sounds—a profound silence. Night was falling; the moon rose in the sky, and still the fox hadn't returned.

More anxious than ever, Fiddle-Fuddle decided to go and look for the fox. The truth is he'd grown quite attached to his host. Ignorant of his dastardly crimes, he still held him as the noblest of beasts. Girding his cloak and drawing up his hood, he walked to the end of the tunnel leading toward the village. Stopping there to pack his pipe, he was about to light it, when he heard soft stealthy footsteps outside. Clearly, it was someone from the village—someone with large, iron-shod boots. Motionless he stood, his pipe in his mouth, flint in one hand, tinder box in the other. The footsteps were coming closer every second; now they had halted at the very mouth of the den. Fiddle-Fuddle put his ear to the wall and listened intently. Suddenly he heard the deep voice of the very blacksmith he'd seen a good while ago at the door of his forge.

"Just you wait, you scurvy villain!" he heard. "The women couldn't smoke you out, but I will! . . ."

There fell a moment of silence. The Gnome's heart pounded in his breast like a hammer, but he didn't remove his ear from the wall, preferring to wait and see what would come. All at once, something irritated his nose so mightily that he sneezed three times in rapid succession.

"Aha! . . . Found you! Snorting already, eh?" spoke the blacksmith's deep voice again. "Just you wait! There's more of this stuff to come!"

Seconds later a great cloud of acrid smoke burst into the passage. The Gnome started back, coughing and choking. A second and third blast followed, and the air inside became so unbearably acrid that tears streamed from the Gnome's eyes.

"That's for my banties! For my roosters! My turkeys!" spoke the same deep voice outside. "Take *that*! . . . And *that*! . . . And *that*! . . ."

And with each *that* a new cloud of smoke burst into the narrow opening, so that the whole passage became dark and quite blue inside. Growing light-headed, Fiddle-Fuddle groped his way back into the den and sought the entrance to other tunnel that led out into the forest, but his head was spinning and it was so dark that, running blindly from corner to corner, he was unable to find it. Cold sweat dripped from his brow; his heart pounded ever more violently. The whole den seemed to whirl before his eyes, and still more smoke was pouring in. Fiddle-Fuddle was already thinking his last hour had come, when at last his hands happened upon the entrance to the tunnel. And dashing through to the exit, he leapt half-suffocated out into the forest where, after running a few dozen paces, he fell among the ferns and lost consciousness.

It was quiet and already morning when the Gnome came to. The smell of burning was still in the air, but the east wind was already blowing it away. He sat down and drew the fresh air lustily into his lungs, but it was a good while before he regained full consciousness, after all, he had a head, and now a very heavy one that kept drooping now on one shoulder, now on the other. When at last he'd fully recovered, he looked back to tunnel exit. The sand was all dug up and blackened with smoke and coal dust. At once, fearing the worst, he sprang up and dashed back to the charred ruins, fearing the worst, for he remembered he'd left behind the goose-quills Greasy Tod that had presented him with, the inkwell he'd fashioned out of an acorn cup, and, above all, the new birch-bark tome, the stitching of which had cost him so much labor. In vain he prodded the sand with a stick to find these items. After a half-day of grubbing about, he retrieved only the blackened stems of the goose-quills. Of the tome remained only a twisted tube with charred leaves on which nothing could be read. As for the acorn inkwell, not a trace!

The hapless chronicler wrung his hands, ruing the destruction of all his hopes; two bright tears rolled down his soot-blackened face. Was this the adventure he'd expected? So! that early morning raider he's heard talk of, that Great Fox, that fearless leader of the Golden Horde who'd plundered the village's poultry yards—could this in fact have been Greasy Tod? So *those* were his nightly expeditions? So he, Fiddle-Fuddle, had aided the fox in his criminal activities? Yes! He had lived under the roof of a cruel robber, and now he shared the punishment for guilelessly trusting a traitor!

The Gnome was still brooding over his cruel deception when the beating of many wings and loud cawing suddenly roused him from his reverie. Looking up, he saw a flock of crows flying overhead toward a hazel thicket where they descended in a black cloud to the ground. Fiddle-Fuddle went to the spot, and there—to his greatest horror!—he came upon the lifeless body of Greasy Tod. The black flock was swarming all over it. Bitter tears shed the honest Gnome over the creature's grisly fate! At last, drawing his hood over his head, he went forth into the world, following wherever his eyes led him.

* * *

Dismal and desolate were the paths he took. The autumn wind blew through the forest, tearing leaves from the trees, carrying

Fiddle-Fuddle would have wasted away to nothing were it not for the groups of children baking potatoes in the stubble fields.

away and tossing them to the ground. The fields turned yellow; the meadows darkened. The last lark had ceased singing long ago. A pale sun peeped through the wracks scudding before the north wind; and in the misty sky you could hear the cry of cranes winging to warmer climes.

Cold and hungry, Fiddle-Fuddle would have wasted away to nothing were it not for the little groups of shepherd children baking potatoes in the stubbled fields. Wherever he saw a thread of blue smoke and a small fire by a forest or in the middle of nowhere, he'd make his way thither, sit down by a pile of brushwood and beg the children for a potato. They were only too glad to share with him, for, while eating, he amused them with all kinds of stories to which they listened open-mouthed.

"Ho! Ho!" he laughed. "I've never passed this way before! So let me tell about the time I was serving in the army—I was an adjutant then. The King and his whole host stood quartered under an old woman's stove. Now one day, we had to march across the hut from the stove to the door. The King sent me, as his adjutant, to ask if we might cross her room. I came out from under the stove, and there she was, sitting at her spinning wheel. Bowing politely, I asked, 'May our army march through your house?' The woman's eyes widened in surprise, but she said, 'You may.' So at once I scampered back to the King. The King signaled to the drummers, and what a clamor broke out under the stove! The band struck up a march, and our entire army marched across the room, saluting the woman with an 'eyes right!' When she told her neighbors about it later, no one believed her."

"Gracious!" said the children, mouths gaping wider than ever. Fiddle-Fuddle tossed more brushwood on the fire, covered the potatoes with hot ashes, and resumed:

"Now, another time, one of our Gnomes was getting married, but he was poor and had nothing to feed his wedding guests. So he went to a sheepdog and said, 'Give me your smallest harvest lamb and I'll invite you to the wedding.' The sheepdog obliged, and soon the groomsmen came to invite him to the wedding. 'Where will the wedding take place?' he asked. 'In the mousehole,' said the groomsmen. 'Fine!' said the dog, and right away he dressed up in a new coat, smeared his shoes with grease, tied a ribbon to his shirt, and went to the wedding. Getting into the mousehole was not easy, but once he'd bent down properly, he managed to squeeze through. What a surprise greeted him there! He thought it would be cramped and dirty inside, but the hall glittered with gold. There was loud music and dancing, the bride and groom took the top of the dance, the table stood set for at least a hundred guests, and the delicious smell of roast lamb pervaded the whole hall. The sheepdog ate and danced to his heart's content. The music even accompanied him home; he sang all the way at the top of his compass. And he remembered that wedding as long as he lived."

"Gracious! . . ." cried the children again, gawking at Fiddle-Fuddle.

"Yes! Yes, my dears!" he said, nodding his head. "Though we Gnomes are small, we are strong and know a good many things."

\* \* \*

Meanwhile, back at Nightingale Dell, Half-Lord had gone out for an autumn walk. His health was rapidly improving. Barely visible now was the scar on his throat where the old woman had stitched up the ruptured skin, and his white cravat covered most of it. Today he was sporting a light-brown riding coat, satin shalwars,[1] a white collar, white cuffs, and a splendid waistcoat from which hung the heavy chain of a pocket watch. He had a cane under his arm, a signet ring on his finger,

---

1   Loose, lightweight trousers, fitted at the ankle; commonly worn in South and Central Asia.

light cracow shoes[2] on his feet, and green gloves on his hands. Puffed up with self-importance he walked, thoroughly pleased with himself, for though he'd lost his voice, he'd since gained twice as much pride, and it was this pride that puffed him up. His fellow frogs hopped on the bank of the stream to look at him. Some croaked in admiration, but Half-Lord never gave them a glance.

"This rabble," he said to himself, "presumes to think it can fraternize with me, associate with me! What brass! As soon as I'm able, I'll get away as far I can from this stream and have nothing more to do with my tiresome kinsfolk. Sometimes people have no idea what to say, or how to say it! Just the other day I met the two bitterns named Marsh-Belcher and Mire-Drum who boast the coat-of-arms *Butor de Butor*,[3] though I contend they spring from common bumblebees. 'Is it true, sir, you come from this stream?' they ask. 'I? From this stream?' I screech, outraged. 'Sirs, not only do I not *come* from this stream, but I cannot *suffer* it, not since the day I was born in it!' That's what I told them. And then if that rabble didn't raise their heads and sing out in unison: 'Boink . . . boink . . . boink . . .' croaked one. 'Ours . . . ours . . . ours . . .' croaked another. 'Frog . . . frog . . . frog . . .' croaked a third.' 'Like us . . . like us . . . like us . . .' croaked a fourth. It was enough to drive one mad! Aye, first chance I get, I'll remove myself as far as I can from these parts! Far as possible! . . . Maybe I'll buy a tenement

---

2  Cracows, named after the city of Kraków, were long, pointed, spiked shoes worn by both men and women from the mid-fourteenth century on.
3  *Butor* is French for "bittern."

house in the city! What with the money I earned from the Gnomes for my beautiful music I have sufficient funds."

As he was saying this, he heard a quiet pleading moan. Looking aside, he saw a wretched little beggar sitting by the fence nearby, bareheaded, face gaunt and wizened.

"Please don't pass me by, sir!" wheezed the wretch, rising to his feet and stretching forth his hand. "I'm a homeless wanderer . . . My name is Fiddle-Fuddle . . . Perhaps you've heard of me? I was King Glistel's court historian . . . I've lost everything, everything, along with my fame for which I sacrificed my peace of mind and happiness . . . Where are my comrades? Where is my country?" As he spoke, great tears fell from his meager face.

The frog, puffing up even more, was about to walk past him, when, suddenly, he saw a magpie bobbing on the fence, looking at him with one eye, then the other. At once the frog changed his mind and reached into his pocket, for he knew that by day's end the whole neighborhood would have learned from the magpie how merciful and generous he was. He reached for the Gnome's hood to drop in his alms, but the sudden movement startled the bird, and it flew away. So Half-Lord changed his mind again. Groping in his pocket for a few bits of dry grass, he took them out and dropped them into the beggar's hood.

"God bless you, sir!" said Fiddle-Fuddle, and reaching into his hood he pulled out a handful of shiny gold sovereigns! Half-Lord gaped in amazement. At once, he thrust his hand back into his pocket where he kept his purse of ducats. Drawing it out, he opened it, only to find it full of dry grass! The frog gave out a piercing screech, as though he'd never lost his voice. Raising his cane he came at the beggar, but the Gnome had vanished. You'd swear he'd sunk into the ground. And all you could hear was a chorus of voices coming from the distant stream:

> *Boink ... boink ... boink ...*
> *Ours ... ours ... ours ...*
> *Frog ... frog ... frog ...*
> *Like us ... like us ... like us ...*

It was the last frog chorus of the season.

# 12

# The Gnomes Retire Underground

The huge, golden autumn sun was setting. Over the past several days, the sky had cleared, the earth had warmed; a fieldfare was warbling its belated song. On the unplowed ridges the white daisies were closing their golden eyes, and the last leaves were falling from the poplars in a great, golden silence. Gelp had just harvested the last of his wheat crop. Bareheaded, clad in a coarse gray smock girded with a linen sash, he stood gazing at the glowing horizon, his face flown with high emotion. On the balk nearby, strong and ruddy-cheeked like two field poppies, his two little sons grazed Gelp's nag; again and again, it neighed as it nibbled on the grass, and the boys' happy little voices rang out in the silence of the sunset.

But in the neighboring dell all was a-bustle with boisterous activity. The Gnome King had summoned his entire company to a final gathering and was about to bring the event to a solemn close. A splendid sight indeed! A royal throne built of field stones, decked with flowers and mosses, stood on a mossy mound under the ancient oak, its leaves trembling lightly in the hushed, radiant air. Around the throne thronged the King's faithful Gnomes, gaily clad, in varicolored hoods, work implements in hand. Here it was all loud chatter and commotion! Not a sad or gloomy face anywhere: laughter traveled from mouth to mouth, eyes sparkled, hands clasped hands fraternally, hearts beat vigorous and loud.

The Gnome King raised his arm; instantly, the hubbub subsided, all murmuring ceased. He was wearing a white robe just as he had worn on that Midsummer's Night Eve; his golden circlet bound his brow, his diamond ball scepter gleamed in his hand. Though his robe was white, the glow of the westering sun fell upon him with such brilliance that the garment shimmered now purple, now gold; his face flamed like fire, and his hoary beard shone like silver. Rising from the throne, he signaled to his bandsmen. They sounded a brief voluntary on golden trumpets, then fell silent. Again the King raised his staff, and gazing down at his loyal Gnomes addressed them as follows:

"My faithful companions! My diligent workers! Your happy days and labors here are over. Eventide falls, and with it comes rest and peace. Gaze upon this past morning and afternoon in the light of the westering sun, for it is the torch that reveals the truth of the day!"

The old King paused, and all was still. Suddenly, a distant sound like the clang of a heavy hammer broke the silence. It was the bell-ringer in the old tower, repairing its long-broken bell, giving it a heart. But the King spoke on:

"It was spring, and you sowed flowers, turning this secluded dell into a happy and beautiful place. It was summer, and you sang songs of peaceful labor. Now autumn is upon us. Behold!

You stand amid her gold and crimson colors, counting the fruits she has brought forth, that you may partake of them with joy."

The King paused, and all was still. Again that strange, clanging sound broke the silence, but this time it was stronger. Louder and louder it beat from the lofty tower. A chill blew over the Gnomes, a chill of shadows, of twilights, of earth's coming harshness. A collective shudder ran through the throng. The King spoke on:

"Behold, a once wild, barren strip of ground was plowed and sown with grain; now it gleams gold in the sunset. See how the soul of the wight, who labored so, rejoices! And you were his helpers. Behold his children! Their little heads once drooped like fading flowers, and now they have been revived. They were sad, now they are joyful. Dark was their future, now it stands brightened. Where there was hunger there will be bread; where there was night there will be dawn. And you were helpers of this light. And behold! There was a little orphan girl: she was homeless, a lamb without shelter, a squab without a nest. Now a roof stands over her head, and the wight has adopted her as his own. A blessing she has brought to the cottage! Goodness flows into it like the fragrance of a spring-time flower. In this, too, you helped with vigilance and grace!"

Again he paused, and all was still. This time the silence was broken by three solemn hammer blows—only three, but so powerful that the Gnomes were left in no doubt as to the finality of the moment. Their annual task on the earth had been accomplished!

The King turned his hoary head and listened. His company listened with him. A shiver ran through them as a cold wind from the forest suddenly blew over the dell. Their bright eyes dimmed, their smiles vanished from their faces, their hands tightened, for well they remembered that old, old saying that wherever a bell tolls, Gnomes must go underground. But the King, undismayed, resumed his address.

"Brothers! We have lost one of our comrades. We have lost our learned scholar Fiddle-Fuddle who left us, seeking worldly fame. It is not for us to judge him. Let him follow his star. But for us, our happy times here are over. Before we depart, let us bless this little corner of the earth."

"Aye, let us bless it!" cried his loyal Gnomes. They fell silent. And raising the scepter in his left hand the old King stretched his right arm over the quiet dell, and blessed it. The diamond ball of his staff shone like a pulsating star. A hundred hands, a hundred arms rose in tandem into the radiant air, and together they blessed that little corner of the earth. And just then the great ball of the sun began its slow roll over the rim of the earth.

"A beautiful sunset!" marveled the King.

"Beautiful . . . beautiful! . . ." repeated his faithful Gnomes.

Suddenly, there fell upon their ears the chiming of church bells. From somewhere far, far off, from regions high above, the chimes came floating down over the forests and woodlands, embracing the fields and meadows; the dewy grasses and herbs trembled. From heaven to earth the bells resounded in the great evening silence. Suddenly, the Gnomes began to shed their vivid colors and hues, even as the trees shed their golden leaves in the sunny blue silence of a September morning, The mossy mound, the throne, the old King and his entire company melted into the shadows. The leaves, floating lightly in the air, fell in a thick layer to the ground, burying the mound where just now the Gnomes had been standing. They would return, but not before the spring sun shone again.

\* \* \*

And what of old Fiddle-Fuddle who was not present at the convocation? Orphaned and forlorn, he trudges through the snow, warming his frozen hands by the moon's silver beams.

Alone in the world roams Fiddle-Fuddle, threading pearls
out of hoarfrost and rime.

Alone he roams, with his hoary beard, his great bushy eyebrows, his hooded cloak, and his honest heart. From his belt hangs a truss of keys with which he locks up the bluebells and maybells, that they might not wake the meadows and groves in wintertime. Alone in the world he roams, threading pearls out of hoarfrost and rime. He has long abandoned all those prideful thoughts of worldly fame which had caused him so much pain and heartache. He has become simple, kind, and unassuming, passing the time with little children and opening his heart to every living creature. True, the news brought to him by Maestro Sarabanda of the twilight and disappearance of his fellow Gnomes dealt him a severe blow, but in time he got over it. Now he can often be seen sitting under an old oak-tree, listening to the songs of a fellow wanderer—a gusli player. He will likely never write his great *History of the Gnomes*. What good to him and the world is a book that flames can reduce to ashes and winds blow away? He has found a much better book—a living book! When little children have trouble sleeping at night, he hops onto their pillows and delights them with tales of the Gnome King Glistel, his golden crown, his royal robe and diamond ball scepter; of the Crystal Grotto; of swords, shields, and knights; of the great spring excursion on Gelp's wagon; of buried treasure hoards, and of Little Orphan Mary and her helpers, his fellow Gnomes. Once, on such a sleepless winter night, he told me the whole story, and this story I have here set down for you, my readers.

## *Finis*

# A Short Biography of Maria Konopnicka (1842–1910)

Maria Konopnicka [pronounce: *kon-op-neets-kah*], poet, novelist, children's writer, translator, journalist, critic, and social and political activist, was born on May 23, 1842 in Suwałki in northeastern Poland, then part of the Tsarist Russian Empire. Her father, Józef Wasiłowski was a lawyer. She was home-schooled and spent a year at a convent pension of the Sisters of Eucharistic Adoration in Warsaw. In 1862 she entered into an unhappy marriage with Jarosław Konopnicki, a member of an impoverished noble family. They had six children. Konopnicka made her debut as a writer in 1870 with the poem, "On a Winter's Morn" (W zimowy poranek). She gained popularity after the 1876 publication of her poem "In the Mountains" (W górach). In 1878, in an unofficial separation, she left her husband and moved with her children to Warsaw to pursue her career as a writer. She often traveled in Europe; her first major trip was to Italy in 1883. She spent the years 1890–1903 living abroad in Europe. In addition to being a writer, she was a tireless social and political campaigner, organizing and participating in protests against the repression of the Polish and Jewish minorities in Prussian Poland. She was also actively engaged in the woman's rights movement. Her literary work in the 1880s gained wide recognition in Poland. In 1884 she began writing children's literature, and in 1888 she debuted as an adult-prose writer with *Cztery nowele* (Four Short Stories). In 1902, in recognition of her great popularity, a number of Polish admirers decided to reward her by buying her a manor house. It was purchased with funds collected by a number of organizations and devotees. As Poland was not an independent country at the time, and as her writings were politically uncongenial to the Prussian and Russian authorities, a location was chosen in the more tolerant Austrian partition of pre-Partition Poland. In 1903 she received a manorial estate in Żarnowiec where she arrived on September 8th. She would spend most springs and summers there, but she would still travel about Europe in fall and winter. She died in Lwów (now Lviv, Ukraine) on October 8, 1910. She was buried there in the Łyczakowski Cemetery.

# About the Translator

Christopher Adam Zakrzewski (born 1948)—literary translator, teacher, scholar. Raised in the UK and Ontario, Canada. Doctoral studies in Russian and Polish literature at the University of British Columbia. Professor of languages and literature at Our Lady Seat of Wisdom College in Barry's Bay, Ontario. Now retired, he and his wife Wendy live in the village of Wilno, Ontario. They have five children and nine grandchildren.